WELCOME TO:
METRAVILLE
POPULATION –
TRYING

these talkies, short stories,
handwritten notes, jokes,
& lists tell the story of
Metraville, well the start
of the story.
Metraville Is! the city's
fresh new slogan.

You may laugh.
Could. Possible.

All the best,
Thanks for your
writing,
Jamie Popowich

METRAVILLE

Jamie Popowich

SEROTONIN | WAYSIDE

INSOMNIAC PRESS

I should have studied kung fu, not ethics.
—Ancient Metraville scrawl

Edited by Jon Paul Fiorentino

Library and Archives Canada Cataloguing in Publication
Popowich, Jamie, 1975-
    Metraville / Jamie Popowich.

Short stories.
ISBN 978-1-55483-032-9

    I. Title.

PS8631.O665M48 2011   C813'.6   C2011-905414-0

The publisher gratefully acknowledges the support of the Canada Council, the Ontario Arts Council and the Department of Canadian Heritage through the Canada Book Fund.

Printed and bound in Canada

Insomniac Press, 520 Princess Ave.
London, Ontario, Canada, N6B 2B8
www.insomniacpress.com

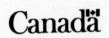  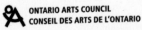

Banana peels everywhere. There's one on your bedroom floor. Another in the closet. Piles of peels on the subway stairs. The doctor prescribes peel pills. Grandma makes broth from them. A husband says to his wife, "Banana peel?" She replies, "Banana peel!" They shout, *"Banana peel!"* as they slam doors to each other's backs.

Meanwhile, gangs keep dyed peels in their back pockets. Gentlemen challenge each other to duels with the slap of a peel. In the candlelit bedroom window across the street, a lecher shows a banana peel to a lady. Two teenagers tie peels to their feet and ride them down a hill. Buildings use peels for curtains. Drugstores sell peels as condoms. Upper crusts wear banana peels as hats. And next year's fall television season is covered in peels.

That man, there, wears peels for pockets. The woman you're about to pass, she uses peels as a bra. A serial killer smothers her victims with banana peels. Hubcaps are diluted peels. Hair is grown from peels. Advice is given out of the stem end of a peel. Small people wear a peel on each ear. Missile silo walls are padded with peels. Cocaine is cut with peels. Eye crust is made up of miniscule shards of peel. Small amounts were found in the blood of the king. Mushroom clouds were shaped in their honour. Science is baffled by the peel's existence.

Banana peels used. Banana peels thrown. Banana

peels fallen. Banana peels sitting. Banana peels waiting. Banana peels peeling. Banana peels banana. Peels banana peels.

Banana peels.

MEET SOME METRA-FOLK

My foot patrols have yet to explain why Metraville has been diagnosed as the city of the future. And what were the ancients thinking when they designed the 'Ville in sectors? All the maps are smudged. Hmm. My wife has left me. Noted. Other thoughts before I fall asleep tonight? From my vantage point, I can safely say that the city sprawl looks beautiful among the night shadows and the silence on the freeway. A pity that the money people keep trying to starve this great place. My home.

    —Batcho "The Butterfly" Alexis, historian, author of *Metraville Landscapes: Crossing Lights, Automobiles, and Skyscrapers, Oh My!*

Metraville has enterprising hearts that make enterprising wallets. Support our dollars!

    —Hal "Everybody's a Pal Of" Grant, Metraville's reigning mayor

"We're going to show you the jasams today."

"The itinerary says 'chasms'?"

"Yeah. The abysses. We got a real problem with them."

    —A conversation with a tour guide

How's that, sonny? Oh, ah. I've lived long in place. We lived before the budget cuts. There used to be balloon rides to get us up steep hills. These were free for children and the aged. I remember my mum just drifting off into the sky on one. We found her a few weeks later living on an apartment balcony. Of course, she paid first and last, so she wasn't able to move back until her lease was up.

    —Pops, Metraville's local colour

Our Daily Affirmations[1]

Miss Smith was shocked when her cat, Jasper, unprovoked, clawed her back. The next week, after a closer examination of the scratches by her doctor, Miss Smith was told that Jasper had clawed her infected kidney. Many people, including the doctor, were sure that Jasper's actions were meant as a warning to his mistress.

They were all surprised three weeks later when Jasper, for no good reason, ate Miss Smith's eyes right out of her head as she lolled in a heavily medicated sleep.

---

1 Daily Affirmations have been a part of the local Metraville colour since the 1940s. Seen as a pick-me-up, like a cup of joe, before the start of a rigorous day. The Miss Smith anecdote comes courtesy of her son, Lionel.

9:15 ● 9:39

Man got a
bumper in the
leg. The car
turning fast enough
to break his
kneecap. People
milled around him
while he rolled on
the sidewalk clutching
at himself, crying.

April 03

2 Manifesto: "I take down the happenings of daily movement then hand-Xerox them myself in ballpoint pen before pushing them into the hands of the stranger-eyes that need to fill themselves as they shuffle."

23:55 ● 00:12

Couple arguing.
hard. Her raking
his face, him
Kicking
her ribs..

August 20

17 : 01   17 : 45

Gorilla-suited
     man lumbers
at pedestrians.
They laughed
until he bear hugged
them. Knocked
their groceries
to the ground.

· June 13

FACE CREAM

(Taken from an interview for the documentary *Behind the Curtains: Vaudeville's Unseen Stars*.)

EXT. ALLEY – DAY

KARL OPPENHUE, dressed in a poncho, black sweater, jeans, rubber boots, runs zigzag through an alley. We only see him from behind.

KARL OPPENHUE (VO)

I inherited cases of the stuff after my grandpop passed on. He bought the entire stock of face cream from a company that he sold for that was going out of business. The company? They were called OTAY Inc. OTAY sold accessories to theatrical shows and vaudeville acts. And my grandpop thought there'd still be a market for the cream, but after he bought the lot, vaudeville went sour and the moving pictures went with a different brand.

INT. CAR GARAGE – NIGHT

KARL sits with his arms hugging his knees. His face is fully covered in cream, but the light is very bad, so we don't completely see him.

> ### KARL OPPENHUE
> Well, me hiding in alleys, that came first. I started using the cream later. And I only started using it because of the alleys. Because when I put that cream on, I can really hide.

KARL moves his face close to the frame. A bit of the cream gets on the lens.

> ### KARL OPPENHUE
> No. Nobody knew about the cream. And I haven't told anyone up until now. I was terrified my dad would find out. By the time I figured out that the cream stopped aging, I was sixteen. He was fifty-three. Can you imagine if he'd known? He would've stolen the lot from me. Then I would have had to watch him stay the same while I got older. That isn't right. You bury your parents, not them burying the kids.

EXT. ALLEY – NIGHT

KARL roams through people's garbage.

KARL walks past condemned house.

KARL walks past rusty cars.

Raccoons walk across the street.

KARL stops walking.

> KARL OPPENHUE
> Ever since I was a child, I thought, "Get to an alley, got to hide." Then I always think, "Got to go." Always like that. First, I think of hiding then of going. And then I do. I mean, look, my parents have been souping me out of alleys since I was four, so I've been doing it a pretty long time.

CUT TO:

INT. BATHROOM – NIGHT

Steam fills the room. KARL is sitting on the toilet seat, applying liberal amounts of cream to his arms. The shower curtain opens. His ex-wife, naked, shakes her arm for a towel.

KARL OPPENHUE (VO)

And, okay, I know some of the triggers. Like there was once I caught a sight a my wife, my ex now, getting out of the shower. But she wasn't mine, you know? She wasn't like how I remembered her. She was sagging some. She said, "Hand me a towel, Trev." Trev? Huh. She never did know me. And I looked at her for a sec more, then I just bolted.

INT. DINING ROOM – DAY

Lights are off. KARL's ex-wife and a small child carry an oversized cake toward KARL. KARL, arms and face covered in cream, sits in a chair in the middle of the room. His family is faintly singing "For He's a Jolly Good Fellow." The cake is placed on KARL's lap. He looks down at the cake and then bolts, knocking the cake—candles still lit—to the ground.

KARL OPPENHUE (VO)

Birthdays are grotesque. And God, holidays. Those nights when the families are all together. The sight of them sends me on an alley-hide every time. Those holidays are always the same. Same memories recapped. Same food eaten. Except everyone's a slight different than the photos show. Line up twenty Christmases of photos and you end up looking at a bunch of people in front of you who look like they're wearing disgusting skin masks.

EXT. EMPTY ALLEY – DAYBREAK

KARL OPPENHUE (VO)
The cream stops me from looking like them.

A line of joggers passes the mouth of the alley. First, one jogger, then a few, then a few more, then one at the back of the pack who is really labouring.

KARL, hiding between two garages, peers around the corner of one.

KARL OPPENHUE (VO)
Of course, I have favourite alleys. I keep a list of them. I've even marked the ones where I've had bad times so I don't go back to them. And there're still a few in the city I've not gotten to. Those ones I'm saving for special occasions.

EXT. ALLEY – DUSK

KARL tries opening a garage door, which is locked. A car turns out of a back drive, its high beams on. KARL, his arm shielding his eyes, backs up and then turns. He walks nonchalantly at first, the car following slowly. As he picks up his pace, the car does as well. Then KARL takes off at full speed down the street.

> KARL OPPENHUE (VO)
> But alleys do make sense. They're full of garbage bins. And garages. You'd be surprised how few garages actually get used properly by people. During bad weather, I've got my choice of at least fifteen garages that, if I went there right now, right this very second, I could stay in for, well, for probably ever without anyone bothering me.

EXT. ALLEY – DUSK – A LITTLE DARKER

KARL hops over a fence. Then he hops back over it. A dog appears a few seconds later, barking.

> KARL OPPENHUE (VO)
> You have to guess how old I am.

EXT. ALLEY – DUSK – ALMOST COMPLETE DARKNESS

KARL pries open the window of a garage and climbs in.

> KARL OPPENHUE (VO)
> Not even close. This face of mine, this face is

twenty-seven years old. My torso, yes that's close to your first guess, but that's only because I decided to stop applying the cream to that part of the body years back because I can hide my body under my clothes. My face, though, people will always be able to see that. So I figure I can let my torso go a bit.

INT. GARAGE – DARK

KARL OPPENHUE

But look at the back of my neck. I was never able to satisfactorily get at that bit. By my reckoning, with the wrinkles, that bit is in its mid-fifties. So, the way I figure, my legs and torso, they'll go first. I don't need them anyway. I'm no athlete. My real feature is my face—that's why I got to keep it young. Once I lose my arms, then I guess the face will go unless I can convince someone to lather the cream on for me. But whom could I trust to do that without nicking the cream for themselves? At the very least, I expect that my face'll last into my late hundred and fifties.

Stalemates

"Where are we again?"

"Let me find out."

"Don't light that match."

"Why not?"

"That was our last one."

"So what? We still have the flashlight?"

"The batteries went out weeks ago."

"I told you not to tell those ghost stories."

"Don't blame me. What about the overhead lamps?"

"They have no bulbs."

"But we packed a box of them."

"We crushed them underfoot."

"Now we'll never get to see where we are."

"That's too bad. I remember I liked the floor."

"It was dusty."

"That was its best feature. I could leave dust prints from one end of the room to the other and still find my way back again."

"It made me sneeze."

"Oh, really? That was from the dust? I thought you had a cold."

"No. I get allergies."

"Allergies? I'll check that off on my clipboard. Have you seen my pen?"

"I haven't even seen your clipboard."

"Neither have I. But I did find the chair."

"I found the chair too."

"I guess our situation isn't so awful then."

"What if I opened the fridge?"

"I'm not hungry."

"Neither am I. But we could use the fridge's light."

"Where is the fridge even?"

"I think it's over there."

"Where?"

"There. In that corner."

"I can't see where you're pointing."

"So what? Are you saying we're never going to get the lights on?"

"That thought makes me feel lonely."

"When did this happen?"

"I didn't see it coming. I was in this chair. You were in that chair."

"Does that mean there's something wrong with me?"

"Are you lonely too?"

"Yes."

"If I breathe loudly, can you hear me?"

"I didn't hear anything."

"I haven't started yet."

"Try again."

"Like that?"

"Sounds to me like you have asthma."

"Why say that?"

"Because your breathing's wheezed."

"Should I get some fresh air?"

"Do you get any?"

"When I feel a breeze."

"Did you just feel one?"

"Yes."

"That was me breathing on you."

"You stink."

"My halitosis must be acting up again."

"I think we should stand up."

"What'll that do?"

"The exercise might cure our breathing problems."

"You first."

"No. I insist. You first."

"It was your idea."

"We should both stand up."

"We'll stand up on my mark. Go."

"Did you stand up?"

"No. Did you?"

"No."

"We try again."

"Why don't we make points first."

"What points?"

"Opinions then. Obviously we both have them."

"We'll both have opinions. And...go...."

"Stand up first?"

"Opinions first."

"Make yours already."

"I won't make my point until you make your point."

"I'm not going to make my point until you make yours."

"Then I'm not going to speak again until you do."

"And me too."

"So am I."

"In one second."

"Fine."

"Fine."

"   "
...

"   "
...

ELEVATOR RIDE

"How's work going up there?"

"Pretty hectic. Last week, they cut the air off in our offices."

"Pardon?"

"I know. They wanted to see what we were made of."

SPACEMAN VOYAGE
TO THE STARS

These are the true space life adventures of Tavis Stiker, Metraville's first citizen in space. This manuscript was originally intended for adults, but due to its short length, it is our suggestion that Mr. Stiker's story is better suited, with the necessary revisions, for children.

by Jamie Popowich

as told by Tavis Stiker

SPACE TRANSMISSIONS (I)

You are a go for orbit.

You are go for orbit.

You all take care now.

the astronaut

has returned to earth

And now his knee hurts bad. This happened on impact with the Earth's atmosphere. The specialists said his body wasn't prepared for the change from microgravity to gravity. *Tavis needed time*, they said. *He just needed time.* And that's all he seemed to have. At 3 a.m., he stared at the clock, his knee keeping him awake. The ache of wake. The never-ending hollow feeling.

The X-rays were no help either. There's nothing there. The doctors held the X-ray up to prove this. Tavis put his finger on the X-ray. It was a side view with no kneecap in sight. How beautiful that was to see, Tavis thought. The cap was gone. In the X-ray, there was no pain. He pressed hard on the darkened space between the two bones.

—There's no break, sir, that's cartilage. That's accounted for. Your knee is a moment of weightlessness caught in our atmosphere.

Fascinated, the doctors giddily ticked off Tavis' reactions as he rode the exercise bike for them. They gave him the thumbs up when he grimaced in the water tank. They high-fived one another when he refused to eat regular food but stuck to the space meals of rehydrated powders and coffee in plastic see-through containers. After much deliberation, the doctors returned with their verdict: space knee.

—Yes, friend, you are still deeply enthralled in space. Finally, someone has brought space home so we can beaker it, ignite it, and weigh its smoke.

Tavis did not share the doctors' glee. He wanted to take a knife to his leg. To delicately slice the flesh off his knee to make a skin-lid that he could lift up. He wanted to unlock his kneecap and then attack the ache. He wanted access to this piece of space stuck in his knee. One hammer punch to that pain and it would surely fart itself all over the room as it deflated.

That's an impossible dream, Tavis thought as he added water to make his scrambled eggs. He limped from the kitchen to the living room without aid of a cane or foolish medication. *Remember, children, all drugs, no matter how good they make us feel, can do harm to a person's body and their marriage.* Tavis pulled his knee to his chest. He imagined the pain, small, unseen, whirling outward through his body, spreading to his movements. The pain covered his thoughts.

His knee was his medically undiscovered country. Above him, beneath him, throughout him. The Space in his leg. His Space pain. Tavis and Space. *Excuse us. Did we say Tavis and Space? Space has got jurisdiction here.*

Space rules. That's the lesson. Space comes first, Tavis a far-off second, that was the pecking order here. No silly Tavis and Space. Space is never second fiddle. Space and Tavis. Space was the main event, Tavis Stiker was the sideshow.

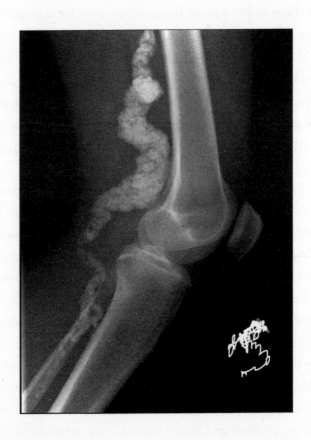

yoga

When people get older, their muscles get stiff. Grans' and Granddad's muscles are the stiffest ever. They probably can't even touch their toes! Yoga makes people flexible.

Tavis the Astronaut does yoga to keep fit. He's the 'Ville's "Cosmic Guy." As a "Cosmic Guy," he has to be the strongest healthiest person in the whole city. He has to walk with his chest out, muscles bulging, always ready to space-hop moon craters.

Like every good city, Metraville wants the Olympics. To promote Metraville, the "Cosmic Guy" was supposed to stand in Spruce Civic Square with a thousand supporters roaring behind him. Can you roar? Tavis sure could.

Then Tavis was supposed to say:

Let's take our first step on the odyssey to gold together.

The whole gang was to take a step. But Tavis couldn't take that step. His knee hurt him too much. Instead, Micro Annabel, the smallest human alive, got to make the speech. Tavis stood three rows behind her, on his best friend Frankie G's shoulders. You can almost see Tavis in the video.

y

    t

       i

           a

                r   v

g

Whee! Floating is fun. Human flying. Weightlessness. Whee!

Gravity is all around us. It keeps our feet on the floor. It leaves our pens on our desks. Gravity lets our mums scold us with wooden spoons and their waving fingers. Most especially, gravity makes sure we're not going anywhere.

In space, there is no gravity. Nothing holds you down to the ground. If you lived on the moon, you would float. Sounds pretty cool, doesn't it? Imagine swimming in the air to go to school!

People don't realize that gravity is what holds us back. Our rocket ships have massive boosters to fight gravity and let us escape into space. "Are people equipped with those boosters?" you might ask. No, of course not. We have to fight gravity with our minds. Gravity is afraid to give up its edge. We can't fight gravity in hand-to-hand combat because gravity holds our hands down. Gravity adds thirty pounds to our bodies, slowing us down, labouring us with excess weight so we can't fight back.

In space, Tavis was feather light. There wasn't any gravity to stop him from getting off the couch. Every step Tavis took was a success. Tavis was the winner against gravity. He won all the time.

SPACE TRANSMISSIONS (II)

We got lightning down here.

Roger. We see the purple cell roving.

How's that?

We see a neon purple worm.

The cloud's roaming for hundreds of miles.

work

Tavis trained for three years in the Hollowman program. He had confidence in himself, in his equipment, and in his team. When it was time to go to space, he was ready to go. Finally, he was an astronaut.

When he came home from space, there was still work to be done. Other experiments had to be conducted. There were new recruits to be trained. On Earth, Tavis catalogued. Tavis monitored. Tavis mission-controlled. Tavis did his duty. **Hooray for the astronauts!**

Tavis' journey into space was recorded. He watches this footage all the time. These were Tavis' contributions to the space program. As his father always used to say to him,

> *You shouldn't look back on your life and regret anything because when you make a decision, you make it on your best judgement at the time. You understand what I'm saying? You got to make a choice, Tavis, with what you know.*

Tavis nodded at his father. Now, before Tavis went to work, he stood in office lobbies watching people go to work, wondering what these people did. What did they think?

Papa, I had regrets. But what happens afterward? Looking back makes sense. But what choices do I make now, Papa? What do I do now?

astrochimps

They were the start of our journey into space. They were the iconic image. Their beaming chimp faces as they were pushed in their special biopack chairs toward destinies with the suborbital. The astrochimps were the true pioneers.

Before Ham the Chimp's trip home, the astrochimps were TOP SECRET. They were named #60 or Chop Chop Chang. A sinister name, that Chop Chop—already on the block. Easy to lose. There would have been a national outcry, a public mourning, for a Ham who didn't make it back to earth alive.

Children adored the astrochimps. Zoo attendance rose dramatically. (Cue Tavis' agent, Mel.) *The children. That's it! They're the ones to sell to. Astrochimps will corner that children's market for you. Don't promote your face, Tavis. Hire a chimp. Picture it!*

astrochimp voyage to the stars

But what about Tavis? Where was Tavis if the chimps took over the story? *Whoa, cool the propulsion, Tavis, you ain't going anywhere. Tavis is still the man. Tavis is still the story. The astrochimp, the Astro-Tavis, why differentiate? Why choose? We love them both. Think of all those impressionable minds chanting,* TAVIS TAVIS TAVIS. *The door swings open.... Wait. Let's not get ahead of ourselves...*

let's savour the moment. There'll be a countdown from 5. We'd make it 10, but the average kid doesn't like to focus for longer then 5 seconds. So 5...4...3...2...1.... Cue swinging door. Kids cheer. Out walks you holding the hand of Tavis the Chimp. No, not just Tavis the Chimp, but Tavis the Twenty-First Century Galatic-Chimp. We lose the word astro, that's a bygone sayonara word.

We have one lucky kid come up for a photo op. You and Tavis shake a couple of hands. Quick stuff. Five-minute stuff. Any longer and we may lose the chimp—he could go apeshit, attack the mob. Those little guys have an unpredictable behaviour. And we hate unpredictable. Unpredictable is scary business. That kind of business kills. We want positive highlights. We want unbridled enthusiasm. We want all this leading to the 3-D live-action extravaganza...

Tavis the Galactic Chimp

versus

The Milky Way

METRACHIMP

figurine

A playset was blueprinted. A Tavis Stiker
model built. One plan had been
to include a small 4 cm by 4 cm
authentic piece of Tavis' spacesuit with
every doll. This idea, the first of many
heartbreaks, was vetoed by all the
various space agencies. Another plan
had been to include asteroid bits, again
kyboshed, this time for fear of possible
alien integration. We should give you a
ray gun, said Tavis' agent, Mel. We'll
sell you as a space defender. But the
toy companies didn't want an outer
space dolly. They wanted shoot-'em-up
"vidyo games." Cops and robbers,
firepeople, doctor, and especially
astronauts, those kinds of careerist
imaginings didn't capture little
Jimmy's and Joanie's minds any
longer. The Tavis doll was binned. A
month later, Mel was selling mountain
excursions to seniors online from his
new basement apartment.

SPACE TRANSMISSIONS (III)

We're all so quiet.

They are a go for landing.

Shhh.

We're waiting for the drop.

space (interview pt. 1)

Have you really been there?

(Tavis doesn't answer the question anymore. He doesn't even blink. You try not to blink. Pretty hard, isn't it!)

Sometimes, when people want to be mean, they criticize other people's achievements. If you've done something you're really proud of then don't ever let someone else trample that. Because they will. They'll put on big, thick, tough boots to squash your accomplishments. They'll sticks-and-stones your feelings with the harshest words you've ever heard. Words like *hoax*, *conspiracy*, *CGI*, and *tax scam*. They'll light your pants on fire, while you're wearing them, to prove the depth of your lie. You'll receive prank calls in the middle of the night from PRIVATE NUMBER. On the other end of the line will be a coward speaking with a voice modulator, telling you he's the extraterrestrial whose probe you enjoyed while sharing packet chicken and mashed potato.

Don't yell when this happens. Don't threaten to call the police. This makes them happy. Do not panic. Put the phone down. Walk away. Roll on the ground. Those are the only ways to keep your dignity. And remember, don't blink. With enough practice, you'll get the hang of it!

boldly going (interview pt. 2)

Do you believe space is our future?

There's no welcome mat in outer space. No red carpet. No birthday invitation.

The moon as getaway home? That charred surface. Please. All those dull craters. Those acres of emptiness. I can't think of anything less hospitable.

Think of the cost of renovations. Contractors would be able to keep them going ad infinitum. Imagine those headlines, "Moon costs keep rising – When will Gran ever get to move in?" Copyrights need to be owned. Sports teams need to fill seats. And the teams? What do you call them? The Moon Raiders? The Mars Attacks? The Dark Siders?

Where's the shopping in space? And without the population, who fills the suburbs? Do we put them on Pluto?

All outer space makes a person feel is small. What can politics gain from that? What's the slogan? You're not insignificant? Space will win that vote. Space will crush that dream.

No. Wait. Maybe there is a way. Earth could have ceaseless wars. Environmental disasters on a worldwide scale. With the right amount of desperation. That's it. We just need the right incentives. That'll get us to space. So, yes, I guess I do believe there's a chance.

SPACE TRANSMISSIONS (IV)

Charlie, it might sound corny, but the view is out of this world.

darkness

Blacken your windows. Turn off your lights. Put a pair of sunglasses on. And last, but not least, close your eyes. Where are the stars? The Earth? And how about your precious sun? That's a fraction of what space is like. That's close to true space. But in space, you begin to wonder when—when will I see light again? If panic sets in,

will I ever see light again?

Imagine the desire to see again. To see freely, without any question, without any fear that the lights will be taken away from you. And I'm not talking about a computer screen. Not a pathetic light bulb either. Those are nothing compared to standing on a downtown street corner with advert video screens on 24-hour rotation. Think of the car headlights, street lamps, street lights, cellphones, storefronts, store signs, bike lights, and the sun at its noonday peak. That's the moment when you realize you can see. I'm not alone. I can see again.

phantom cosmonauts

(NOTE TO TEACHERS – This is an ideal section for the study of space exploration)

A number of astronauts were sent into space as experiments, or the more scientific label of *guinea pigs*. For decades, there were rumours of lost cosmonauts [Editor's note: a Russian astronaut] left floating in space because of their experiments. Bodies against the darkness. Their suits intact. The Russian fibres winning one of the Cold War battles. If those cosmonauts were up there, drifting without a home, the wear and tear of atmosphere degradation meant that the flesh and bone would have long ago fused and disintegrated.

But where were those phantom cosmonauts? Tavis never saw them. Where were those deflated bodies whose minds were done with travel but whose suits still rippled across the universe in voyage?

SPACE TRANSMISSIONS (V)

The crow is nested.

I repeat: the crow is nested.

brother eddie (a phone call)

Tavis, you're a dependable guy. When I call you, asking, "What should I do about...?" "Should I keep living with...?" "If I steal that wall, will I...?" Tavis, you listen to me. You give me good advice. You've seen the stars, man. You've been on the cusp of the universe. And sure, maybe light speed was unattainable. Maybe that Martian technology was out of reach. Like, I don't know. But I know you're a big part of the ball rolling. That's why I come to you today. You got to figure me out. I'm a Frankenstein looker. I got left feet for brains. I can't hold no conversation with a person. Speaking is a maze that I can't get out of. You hearing me, chief?

Eddie, I can't lend you any more money.

I'm not even asking for nothing. I'm talking. Only talking. Can you just talk to me? Can you talk me out of my brain maze? Can you do that at least?

What am I supposed to talk you down from? Have you climbed on someone's roof? Are you up another tree?

Naw. No tree. I'm chilled, man. Completely chilled on that score. I can't even walk. Can't even step forward. Imagine if Papa saw us now. Me, the genius who can't figure out even a metal rod. You, the spaceman without your suit.

You'll solve yourself. I know you will.

No point, Tavis. Sometimes you got to let life be a mystery. You get me? Leave the unknown unknown.

Is this where I'm supposed to change your mind?

No way. Crapademics is fini. I'm talking about my kisser today. I'm talking about my zig-zaggetty brain. I want you to guide me. Draw me up a path. Tell me to throw out my mirrors. Write me instructions for Monday to Friday. I'll follow your lead.

But I'm lost.

What? Oh, shit. Come on. Is Tavis Stiker there?

Eddie?

Is Tavis there?

Eddie, it's me. I'm here.

Tavis is that you?

We've been talking this whole time.

Shoot. I hoped I dialed the wrong number.

Why?

Then I'd still have a brother to call.

EARTHLY
TRANSMISSIONS (I)

He's a doll?

Sorry, are you talking to me?

Your date. He's the size of a doll.

granny

Granny was always up the tree in front of her bungalow. Tavis and Eddie would go over to her house to see if she'd eaten that day, and if she hadn't, one of them had to climb up and give her some food.

—Did you get my email? she asked.
—No, Gran.
—It must still be there on the grass. Don't know why it didn't send. Order me Moonglow. They'll deliver. There's money in the cigar box by the chesterfield.

Tavis picked up the crumpled piece of green construction paper off the lawn as he went into the house. It read:

To: Tavis & Eddie
From: Gran
Re: Food.

   Chinese.

Gran told her stories while they ate in the tree.

My brother, Teddy, was thirty-one when he drowned. Went to a birthday party and the boat they were in cracked in half. He always said he was going to retire young. He retired young alright.

The youngest, Percy, he drowned too. We couldn't find his body for two weeks. When we did, the fish had eaten his eyes and all his hair. The eyes I understand, but why the heck did they eat his hair?

Exploration is beautiful, boys. The seafaring is the only life worth anything.

friendships

—Oh, Tavis. I don't know how I'm going to pay my bills.
—That's too bad.
—The bank doesn't want to give me a break. Can you send me some dough?
—I'm broke. (He's not.)

—Tavis, look at this website. People download the most hilarious things.
—(Tavis fakes laughter.) Like what?
—Like this monkey pushing this elephant into a river. Now where is it? Shoot. I want to show it to you. I can't find it. I'll have to send you a link.
—(Tavis stops smiling.) Don't bother.

—Have a good night, Tavis. Don't work too late.
—I wasn't going to.
—Yeah. I know you weren't. I was just saying.
—Do you think I work too hard?
—Relax. It's just something people say.
—I don't say it.

—Mr. Stiker, your account is up to date.
—Is that good?
—You're one of our best customers.
—I wish I wasn't.

—Hey, mister. Would you pass us our ball back?

—Get it yourself. I don't want to cross the road.

—But we're only children.

—That's your problem.

—Are you mean because you're a lesbian?

—No, I'm a man.

reunion

Are you married?
> When is she expecting?
>> Ha, ha, same old Marty Baker!

>> I can't believe we did that.
> Feels like a dream.
Do you remember when...?

EARTHLY
TRANSMISSIONS (II)

People who work in a cigarette factory will say,

"Well people have to relax."

People who work in a missile factory will say,

"Well, we need a strong defense."

f
a
l
l
i

n

g

Tavis could never escape the feeling. His feet never felt at rest on the floor of the Nervous System. If the ground had opened up, if those vibrations, those shake-rattles, had escalated, he would have dropped out into space. He was one massive malfunction away. Here an inch, there an inch, everywhere an inch inch. Reminds him of a couple of acrobats from a picture magazine he'd seen who walked a tightrope stretched between two peaks of the Alps. Under them was six thousand feet of nothing. The acrobat bodies might be puzzled back together, his could not.

No matter where Tavis put his feet, he could feel the vibrations. He couldn't shake the feeling—behind his back, the jerking of his calf muscles—that underneath him was nothing. Nothing to grab onto in freefall. There would be no depth perception either. With nothing around him, no trees, no buildings, no balconies rushing by, Tavis would have no idea that he was falling. With nothing to see, there was no way to tell.

On impact with the ground, there would be no store awning to break his anything. Tavis would be gone completely forever.

s
i
n
e
p

Tavis couldn't get his cock hard. No blood circulating that way. Don't dare mention blastoff around him. Don't ask if he drinks Poon-Tang. Tavis wasn't boldly going anywhere.

–*Doctor, what am I going to do?*
–*Vell, some times da penus does not vant to do da vork.*

Why was this happening? Atmosphere change. Stress. Work. Space travelled. Throw those at a full-blooded male; they'll turn him half-blooded in a hurry. Why not throw the galaxy at Tavis as well? Swing the Big Dipper at his crotch. Get Gemini to crush his sac.

Menu for a Hard Cock

To Fix That Old Soft Problem:

Take lubrication
View a stimulating exchange of pornography
Close eyes and remember your most precious sexual encounter

Make sure to rub furiously

(cue song)

rub and tug, watch and think, look at member
    shrink-a-dink

Not shrink-a, damn it. Little member hard and thick.
Even the song was failing Tavis.

—Doctor, please!
—If all else fail, telephone ze professional.

PROFESSIONAL HELP BELOW!

"Oh, baby. Tell Buffy what you like."
"I like girls," said Tavis.
"You want me to get my girlfriend?"
"I'm saying I like girls."
"I'm a girl."
"For real?"
"Oh, yeah, sugar-top. I've got the wet pussy passport to
prove it."
"Your voice sounds low."
"You want my mouth on your hard-on?"
"Do you have tits only?"
"And a tight asshole."
"I said I only like girls."

"Listen, motherfucker. We're only talking. Can you dig that? What the hell does it matter about my dick?"

"Is it hard?"

"Not for you, you weak-muscled pin."

EARTHLY
TRANSMISSIONS (III)

Oh no. What are you doing here?

You should be happy to see me because I'm F-U-N. Capital Fun!

(canned laughter)

That's what I was afraid of.

(more canned laughter)

sleep

Tavis pushed away from his computer toward the cor-
ridor. He floated over wires, cords wound five deep
around the circular halls, and then he shook the green
mesh athletic bags to make sure they were securely tied
down. He stopped before another computer station to
monitor its progress.

> —How's your sector, Frankie G?
> —You still here?
> —I never want to leave.

*Wakety wakety. Let the confusion wash away like
the tide from the beach. Come back into yourself.
You are here. Be here. Think here. Want here.
Chubby neck. Pudgy fingers. Thick body. Find fat
feet. Stand. Release.*

Tavis gripped the subway train bar. Space station
Nervous System was today, he thought. Like the old
saying goes,

> *Today again, to-gone again, to-bye again.*

Disturbance. Restlessness. Dancing bed legs.
Lumpy pillows. Hot room. Cold air. Caffeine
too close to beddie-bed. These were the con-

founders of Tavis' sleep.

On the Nervous System. He was living life. How did he get here? Was it teleportation? Had he discovered time travel? Is this the dream?

 —*I'm so late.*
 —*There's always time, said Frankie G.*
 —*But it took so long to get here.*
 —*Don't worry. We have until seven thirty ante meridiem.*
 —*We have before noon?*
 —*We're in space. We have our own clock.*

Tavis' alarm bleeped. Tavis pushed against people as he got on the subway. He rubbed his eyes. He yawned. Before Beacon 1 launched into space, his crew sat in their chairs for hours, waiting, knowing that at any second the mission could be called off.

Spaceflight participants, abort mission. We repeat: abort mission.

They also knew that airplanes, they go up, they land. With rocket ships, the odds weren't as definite. No one fell asleep waiting for lift off.

The rocket was shaking. Is this how it feels? Is this how it sounds? An image passed before Tavis' eyes.

Within his grasp, another image came into focus. He forgot the previous one. Another image buried under an image under an image. He couldn't escape them. They were his present movements.

He pushed toward the subway doors again.

Where was he?

EARTHLY
TRANSMISSIONS (IV)

Hello, Ping.

Where Bob, Fat Girl?

About that, I've got bad news.

(silence)

Bob doesn't want to marry you anymore.

"Live your life and have many experiences."

That's what Tavis was told to do and that's what he did. He lived. He climbed mountains. He swam in oceans. He slept with many women. He knew the company of ladies. In college, he was the Tav-Man. He lived life up.

Then he went into space. He was on his spacewalk when he found his speck. He pressed his baby finger on it. Caught you, he thought. Though he was sure the speck would fall off while he was working. If the speck lasted, surely it would disappear when he got into the antechamber. But the speck was still on his glove after his spacesuit was sprayed clean.

Tavis didn't tell anyone. He put his bare hand over the speck, took it to his bunk, and hid it in the box where he kept his father's wedding ring. There were rules to follow. You can't bring anything back. Absolutely no souvenirs. No stopping at the Astral Duty Free. Tavis knew this. He knew that the speck could be an unstoppable flu virus that would spread across the planet killing millions of people. My speck is a mere nothing. But he didn't want to believe it. Instead, he thought, the universe would never miss it.

He couldn't keep his speck to himself. He showed the speck to people.

—There's nothing there, chief.

—Where'd you really get your spacesuit, a garage sale?
(laughter)

—Did you ever get to the moon?
—No, said Tavis.
—Big deal then. Planes practically get you to space as it
is.
—But what about my speck?
—I don't see anything.

Tavis opens his hands. He saw his speck. The speck
existed. He cupped it in his hand under bright lights,
marvelling at his find. Here was proof that he'd been
to space. Seven years is a long time ago. That time was
disappearing. The speck was his truth. His speck.

the planet earth

Perspectives change when the whole planet's in view. Regular people see the whole world in crumbs. They see toothbrushes, the tree out front of their home, the street block they walk down, and the building they work in. That's not the magnification of space. I was one hundred fifty thousand miles away from Earth. Everything I know—my family, my friends, my possessions, my country—they're so insignificant in relation to space. Only an astronaut gets to travel the bridge between Earth and the moon and understand its vastness.

From my stool, I looked out at Earth every day. I saw the full shape of time. There were no more dinosaurs, Roman Empire, or World Wars. What had gone, what was to come, those ruins we've made of our stories. Those blips are mere nothings. Moments of erosion. All part of the shifting make-up of the planet face.

I was outside all this. Outside that port window was a conversation I'd never had before. A conversation I wasn't having. You can't talk to Earth. But it was speaking to me. In all the buzzes of our work, I heard the silence. And in the silence, Earth spoke to me

you are outside now

EARTHLY
TRANSMISSIONS (V)

"But you're seven feet tall! How did you ever ride a pony?"

(children giggle)

"I just remember having a pony and then not having a pony."

"What? It went that fast?"

"Yeah, it was like a week."

(audience laughing and clapping)

"I can't believe you're laughing at my equine misfortunes."

(more laughter)

orbiting routines

shower every day
brush teeth
breakfast
lunch
dinner
sleep at eleven
fill hours with work
watch figure at all times

journal entry

Tavis writes this remembrance every day: "Thirteen days in space. Sailing personnel of the universe—eat the fruits and vegetables quickly. Typically, dinner eaten with crew. The assignment: to use the robotics app. There are no records to be set. There were physicals, vomit comet rides, psychological scans, committees of judges. We had technicians, all those men and women who monitored us, talked with us, made sure our world was kept as normal as possible.

After de-orbiting, on wobbly legs, Earth rocked, my body completely dehydrated. I took my spacesuit, my workaday clothes, off for the last time."[3]

---

3 Scientists put 30-1 odds that Tavis can put himself back together. They could have made the odds much higher, but then nobody would have placed a bet. Tavis' sanity wasn't a bet the chancers were chomping at. The real money was riding on the Halley's Comet appearance. The popular betting date was August 17, 2061. Though Halley's apparent magnitude, the proliferation of dead satellites discarded in space, and gravitational pull were all keen factors affecting the odds hither and thither.

galaxy missing

I'm standing in front of a department store change room mirror. Kids are struggling outside with their mums. Fathers stand against walls, fretting over costs. The perfume-sprayed air soaks into all our skins. I press my nose against the mirror. I don't want to look at my receding biceps. I detest my bloated belly—no matter how many sit-ups I do, my belly won't flatten. I still shave off my pubic hair—the polite shave, as I used to tell women—but I should grow the hair back and stop exposing how lonely I am. I don't want to watch any of this. Where in my sunken eyes is Tavis Stiker? Have you seen him? Who am I talking to? Tavis Stiker. Where is he? I'm right here. Who? Tavis. Tavis Stiker. Oh, you're Tavis Stiker? Yes, I'm Tavis Stiker. I've got the right number then? You do. I am Tavis Stiker. I am he. Am I? Am I Tavis Stiker?

METRAVILLE

X

Commercial Fare

Anyone out there? Anyone at all? Anyone suffering from deprivations of the somnambulant kind? Are your eyes sagging cheekward? Slipping, sliding, past bone to mouth's corners? Come on. You know what I'm discussing here. Being there. Being here. Being home. All those *being* cards shuffled ecstatically. The head spun so far round that where the start point is is where the day began and the places between the places, all non-remembered. Stumbling. Crawling. Travelling. Forward. Holding your back up. Use your hands to avoid a worse crooked frame. The pain of movement! The answer is simple—

BREAKING NEWS
Building Jumps off Man

"We're going to have to leave this breaking news, Doctor John, to bring you breaking news. This breaking news just breaking now. We're going straight to the east end of Metraville, where Jim Rord has a breaking story. Jim, what's happening?"

"I'm standing in chaos and fear. Only moments ago, at the corner of Richmond and York, Building One Thirty-Two committed suicide. An architect had been on the roof at the time, trying to coax the building down, but as you can see from the devastation around me, he was unsuccessful."

"Jim, do we know how this started?"

"Well, Jim, workers tell me that around six this morning they noticed Building One Thirty-Two start to sway far to the right. Many hoped wind was a factor, but a sanitation worker just told me that the reason the architect was called so quickly was that One Thirty-Two was seen as a risk to itself, and that over the past four months, some cubicles and two small offices in the building had already plunged to their destruction."

"Jim, do we know yet what caused One Thirty-Two to jump?"

"Workers familiar with the site are telling me that One Thirty-Two had been going through major renovations for the past year, and that the renovations were not going according to schedule. Apparently, cost cutting may have played a major part in this tragedy. And right now, what most fear on the street is that other copycat buildings will follow suit. Meanwhile, rescue crews are hoping that they may be able to salvage some intact walls or, if they're lucky, maybe they can find a whole floor. I'm told that this has happened in the past."

BUY LOCAL

"And how much is that?"

"You want it severed?"

"Could I purchase it still intact?"

"I'm not sure. Hold on. Hey, Harold. Harold?"

"What?"

"Do we got any left that aren't severed?"

"They're on back order."

"Got a guy on the phone here who's wondering how long that will take?"

"It's on back order."

"Harold doesn't know. Once it's on back order, it's out of our hands."

"You can't even give me an estimate?"

"I'm not asking him again. He's in a bad enough mood. Take the severed. That's just as good."

"But now I'm fixated on an attached—"

"I hear you. I really do. But I don't want you to have to go without."

"I can wait."

"You'll wait?"

"Oh, definitely."

"Harold, he says he'll wait."

"That'll cost him fifty clams."

"Harold, what's the money for?"

"For the deposit. No clams, no magic."

"How far down the list would I be?"

"Harold, how big's the list?"

"I'm trying to run a shop here. Tell him if he wants to know so bad to come down."

"Harold, come on. He's a bit of a cripple."

"I'm not."

"Shut up."

"If he puts down a hundred, he'll be second."

"Harold says if you—"

"I heard him."

"Harold likes cripples. That's why I said it. Are you going to put down money?"

"Absolutely. What if I put down more? Then can I be first on the list?"

"No."

"Why not?"

"Harold's always at the top. Count yourself lucky that he's putting you second. My wife is tenth."

"What about you?"

"I get my fill at work."

"What would you recommend to tide me over?"

"I can set you up with a ten-pound bag of legs and foreheads."

"Is that two bags?"

"No. It's a mix."

"Okay. I'll do that."

"I just need your address and a payment method and then I'll get this over to you.... Harold, how long to get a ten-pound delivered?"

"For the cripple?"

"Yeah."

"I'll do it tonight."

"What do I do? He'll see I'm not a cripple."

"Harold, you've got to leave it on his door."

"So, I'll leave it on the door."

"He'll leave it on the door." (whispers) "If I were you, I'd crawl to the door to pick it up."

"How will I get the door open?"

"Use ingenuity."

"Okay."

"Alright, sir. Your legs and foreheads will be there tonight."

"I really appreciate your help."

"Don't mention it. I've been having a bit of luck today. Felt I should spread some sunny joy."[4]

---

4 Available at any of your finer *meat* shops.

A Metraville Sandpits Weather Update

And now for your daily outlook. Parents are being warned to keep children under two inside for fear that weighted raindrops might warp their soft skulls. This warning is also in effect for seniors over the age of sixty-seven, all house pets, and the generally marginalized.

If you're planning a day out at the Metraville lakeshore, you're being asked to watch for space junk. Be sure to report any sightings, noting time and location, and make sure to contact the Junkists immediately. Failure to do so may result in fines or criminal prosecution. This footage sent to us from Dinah and Ger Lewiston, of Metra Avenue One/Fifth, is their discovery of the body of a cosmonaut during their annual picnic. Remember, folks, while funny now, don't follow Ger's tragic example and touch or try to impress your family by wearing the space junk.

Be wary of terminal amounts of sun in the lower sections. This will be followed by flash sewer rushes and intermittent spitting.

And finally, tonight, the infrastructure of our tall buildings is on the brink, so please step lightly when doing your shopping or working your 9 to 5.

a recovered email—found during an internal investigation into the activities of several senior city officials

1. Search the web
2. Change identity
3. See what is what is what
4. Intersurge with other accounts
5. Run away

▨jazzmail

chimmylong@jazzmail.mv

Your point about terror action—that's the kind of catalyst we need in the city—that's so full power. Other cities get diseases, dictators, floods, commies. What has Metraville? We need a bang-bang. An event worth the price of admission. Something that will tag Metraville with BREAKING NEWS. Then we can get ourselves some star-fire behind us. We'll get a national anniversary. We'll get mourners. We'll get children from the other side of the planet with tears for our Metra-folks. Then we can clear the highways, because here come the trucks full of tax dollars. The house prices will blow up. And all those houses will be empty because of the people's exodus from the city. And in the meantime, we gobble up the lands as fast as our hands can take hold of 'em. All because of the new pumping hope, from tragedy, to the revitalizing, to the rebirthing of the city.

1. PackRatted (1)
2. Dump
3. Incompletus (1)
4. Pigeoned Off
5. Buried (12)
Say hello on jazzenger (Web)
Press GO from this location

A question for the ages that keeps audiences guessing —
what what. But what what of who who? Disagreements
have surfaced about the validity of who who, but if put
to the test, who who is what what we're always asking.
Examine. Who who is on the phone? Who who am I
dating? And of course, who who took the pie off the
windowsill? Dig deep who who. Dig deeper who who.
Where where is who who? What what has who who
done? And why why is who who holding that knife? See.
Who who. Feels right, right? Try it sometime. You'll find
it was always there. You've just let who who and what
what collect dust.

YOUR DAY IN COURT

(Preceedings Underway in the Case of PIERCE vs. DONALDSON APB; PCP; TNT)

MR. PIERCE: I wish to correct a statement I made during discovery.

MR. DONALDSON: A correction to what?

MR. PIERCE: To the question, did I have a fax machine.

MR. DONALDSON: And what is it you wish to say now?

MR. PIERCE: Before...when I stated that I didn't have a fax machine...I meant to say that I have a fax machine.

MR. SOUTH: So you're saying you have one?

MR. PIERCE: Yes. I have a fax machine.

MR. SOUTH: This is outrageous, Your Honour. This completely changes our case.

YOUR HONOUR: How so?

MR. SOUTH: Well, clearly if he had a fax machine...I mean he has one....

YOUR HONOUR: I'm sorry, counsel, but I don't understand where you're going with this.

MR. SOUTH: Where I'm going is...has he used it? Does he know how to use the fax machine?

YOUR HONOUR: Well, Pierce? Can you use the fax machine?

MR. PIERCE: I mean mostly the, uh, the receptionist would send out my notes. But, yes, I could use it.

YOUR HONOUR: Look, Mr. South, I have no problem with Mr. Pierce owning a fax machine. Mr. Donaldson, does this change anything for you?

MR. DONALDSON: No, Your Honour.

MR. SOUTH: If it pleases Your Honour, I wish to retract my last statement.

YOUR HONOUR: That seems reasonable to me.

MR. DONALDSON: I have no problem with that either.

YOUR HONOUR: Then please strike the prosecutor's last statement. Carry on, Mr. Pierce.

MR. PIERCE: Thank you.

LESSON

There was a man who brought weather daily to the men. They hugged and kissed his forehead as he passed out storm clouds, sunrays, and mud showers. Once his pockets were bare, he walked back to the warehouse to collect more. He did this without complaint.

Momma-A-Go-Go

Julian Baxter and his defense lawyer, Vronsky, were in the defendants' closet waiting to be called out for the verdict. Vronsky tried to pace with a swagger, but because the closet was so small, he ended up hitting his head against one wall and stubbing his toe on the other.

"How long will they keep us here?" asked Julian.

"Stuffy, yeah? I wonder how much the air weighs."

"Why would you want to know that?"

"For analysis of smog."

"How is a stuffy closet going to explain smog?"

"Maybe closets produce smog. Maybe cow dung is not the great environmental disaster we've always feared."

"Is there a major fear of cows?"

"I represented a farmer. He ended up doing the hardest time, but no matter. He told me all sorts of facts about moo-bombs, udder-guns, and basic cow digestion. You'd be surprised what you don't know.

"Wait. Shh." Vronsky pressed his ear against the door. "I thought I heard tapping. Oh, God, Vronsky, don't faint again. Stay upright. You got food? Water?"

"The guards confiscated all that when we came in," said Julian.

"They're not supposed to do that."

"You told me to hand it all over."

"You gave them the picnic basket?"

"Yes."

"That's what they were eating from during the case. That looked so delicious."

"We'll never know."

"Those guards scare me. I've seen them do—shh. Can you hear talking?"

"No."

"Do you think they're talking about us out there?"

"Probably."

"Would that constitute talking behind someone's back?"

"I don't think that's exactly what it means."

Vronsky whispered, "Could I sue them for being inflamed toward me?"

"I don't really know the law."

"I hear you buddy."

Three loud knocks rattled the door.

"Marchie's staff," said Vronsky. "This is it. Before we go out, listen: I'm sorry if this doesn't go according to plan."

"Thirty minutes ago, you were confident."

"Was I? Shoot. I wish I felt that way now."

Judge Stone's court would have been packed regardless of the energy shortages, which, yeah, there were, or if the price of admission were reasonable, which the rates definitely were. The audiences went because when a man such as Judge Stone brought down law—really, when he brought down his form of the law—people had to be there. They had to watch Stone's lips as he was stating Stone Law. They had to listen for Stone Law. Call them witnesses, participants, followers, believers, disciples—there was a different classification and a different reason for what drew each of them to the court.

The court had been an abandoned school gymnasium until Judge Stone grabbed ahold and made it into his reclamation project. He'd set up pews for the first three rows of the audience. Sitting in a pew would cost a person five bucks—with the five bucks getting a person a twenty percent discount on the lunch. The cheapest way going was for people to bring their own chair. The cheapies sat behind the pews and were where the majority of the audience pitched down. The crowd in this part of the audience was known as the Bringer's Mob.

Lawn chairs were the seat of choice for the Bringers,

being the lightest and most portable, but there were some regulars, those ones who had airs about their stature within the court, who made an effort to sit in a finer make of seat. Regulars could be easily identified. They were the ones sitting in rocking chairs, recliners, or on the occasional chesterfield. One couple was even known to bring a loveseat to snuggle in.

The lawyers also had to supply their own seats. But their seats didn't pan out like the audience's. An old-time lawyer wouldn't splash out on a souped-up chair. Those lawyers went for simplistic, maybe a tree stump or a pillow. The rookies were the ones who brought expensive show pieces to try to make a big splash. They had their schmancy car seats, their leather chairs, or plush fainting couches.

A defense lawyer such as Vronsky went for the more *unconventional seating method* (these being his words). Vronsky believed in standing for questioning, the squat while listening, crossed-legs-on-the-floor if the case was going long, and steadfast pacing back and forth for opening, closing, and sentencing. The word amongst the veteran members of the audience was that Vronsky's affected style wasn't style at all, but style from necessity. Because everyone knew that Vronsky was one of those dead-pool lawyers. He was a lose-lawyer. A case-bomber. A sentencing-malfunctioner. Whatever Vronsky told his clients, whatever spin he spun about his lack of chair-wear, that was down to the loss column, and the loss column led to broke accounts that led to the seatless attorney, which led right to Vronsky.

Vronsky's law was empty pockets and seat-of-the-well-worn-pants practice. At this point in his career, all he could play out for was the lawyers' pension that was doled out to the thirty-five-year vets of the war on justice. And none of his peers resented him grasping for that achievement. Everyone felt a bit sorry for Vronsky and his inabilities. And they'd have felt much worse for him if he didn't help with their win percentages.

Take the case Vronsky was dancing with Stone over today. Another low-end bungling burglar job that Vronsky always got glued to. The kind of case where no prosecution was necessary. Just Vronsky and Stone in a battle over how guilty Vronsky's client was. Vronsky was there to try to stop the guilt getting out of hand. That meant Vronsky had to keep up a cool, thinking, listening, and watching head, without snoozing. Because if he could step through Stone's land-mind maze without tripping up, well then, Vronsky's guy had a chance. Then his man, Julian Baxter, might avoid Stone Law being thrown Stone-Speed at him.

From his swivel chair, Stone looked down at Vronsky and Baxter.[5] The Baxter case had been going

---

5 In Stone court, there was no bench, no gavel, no stenographer. Years ago, Stone successfully sued the courts for the right to brand his own justice. Stone wanted an open concept with a swivel chair mounted on three risers. Stone wanted no surprises. No hidden agendas. Just Stone as Stone. Now, his assistant, Marchie...

on for four days. That was four days of Vronsky brouhaha. Seventeen witnesses. Three Vronsky closing arguments. Baxter's insufferable weeping mother.

Stone was tired. Stone was drifting. Stone was plain bored. He took a lozenge from the breast pocket of his judge's garments. He popped the lozenge into his mouth, slurped softly once, and then slurped hard. As he did this, he kept a steady gaze on Baxter. Stone snapped for Marchie, who stepped up the three riser steps to Stone's chair. Marchie raised the stainless steel plate he'd been carrying under his arm to Stone's chin and waited for the PING. The nearly evaporated lozenge, surrounded by a mound of spittle, landed on the plate. Marchie then handed Stone a white handkerchief, which Stone used to dab himself off. Then Stone waved Marchie away.

As one, the crowd leaned forward, their ears tilted toward Stone. Mrs. Baxter, Julian's mum, lifted several tissues to her eyes. The lozenge, Marchie, the handkerchief: all signs that Stone was ready for judgement. His throat was lubricated, his face clean of blemish.

Marchie was a puzzle to the Stone regulars. They didn't understand what Marchie was supposed to symbolize, though the Marchie name had been passed from one waif-framed elderly man to the next who was hired when the previous one passed away. Amongst the regulars, there had been a longstanding rumour that Marchie was in fact a salute to Stone's much loved, but departed, father. And the Stone disciples only thought this because Stone had once beckoned a Marchie over by saying, "Da. Here. Da. Here now."

("Symbols," Stone always said, "go a long way to sending a straight message out to those crooked crooks.")

Vronsky gripped Julian's hand. "For once, I have a good feeling," he whispered in Julian's ear.

"You done chatting?" asked Stone.

Vronsky bowed his head in reply, biting his tongue as he did so, knowing that anything he said would only sink Baxter further in the pits.

"So, Baxter," said Stone. "Like countless criminally minded peers that have come before you, you eventually got jammed by authority. You rode high until you got dashed down. You thought you were slicker than the rules. Nuh-uh, pal. You're not invisible. You can't fit between the cracks in doors. You can't even sneak through keyholes. We have a defense against people like you. And I'm not talking about the coppers. I'm not speaking of the law. I'm talking here of community, of citizens who linked, arm in arm, to have you dredged up from the sewer.

"You came into our community. My community. You burgled us. You burgled me. Then, to kick us further, you have Vronsky here try to convince me of your good character. Vronsky asks me to go easy on you because you made some wrong choices. Let me ask you: Do Right Choices join syndicates? Do Right Choices steal from the innocent? And I know, I know—Right Choices aren't always perfect, right?" Stone swept his eyes around the court. "I don't think so. Good characters like my community, like myself, we earn our living the old-fashioned way."

Vronsky was beside himself. He couldn't hold back. "By old-fashioned, do you mean bribes, Your Honour?"

No one laughed. Many of the audience, having been here before with Vronsky, held their heads in their hands.

"Is that a joke?" asked Stone.

"Just trying to cut the tension, Your Honour."

"And this cutting of yours, do you find that it's very helpful?"

"Well, the way I see it, Judge Stone—"

"Vronsky, you're a blind idiot who sees nothing. You stumble around fingering cooked spaghetti and bowls of grapes, thinking that you've touched brains and eyeballs."

"Stone, you got to understand. Guys like Baxter and me, we didn't grow up with the kind of chips that guys like you got stuffed in your breeches. Our tooth fairies didn't give us bank deposits, they came and stole from us. See, without the riches, Baxter and me, we couldn't educate ourselves and build up such great character like you got."

Julian jabbed Vronsky in the ribs. "You've said enough," he said.

"What's the problem? I'm arguing for you here."

"You're not helping," said Julian.

"Oh, but he is, Baxter, he is," said Stone. "Vronsky-Man, you've put your finger on it. Vronsky has touched the crux that I could only graze over in my mind while I was sitting in my chambers. Vronsky, you're like a piece of dynamite blowing up in people's faces, and for once, you've blown up properly."

"Thank you, Judge Stone. That means a lot coming from a guy like yourself."

Judge Stone didn't even pay attention to him. "See, Baxter, Vronsky asked, in his own mishandled way, the most pertinent question of them all. Because whose fault is all this really? And by 'all this,' I mean your own befuddled life. Why did you end up a back alley thief? Was the crime manager the problem?" Stone motioned to Tugs Shandy, Julian's boss, who sat in the front row. Tugs bowed, happy to finally be included in the proceedings. Though the only reason he had even shown up in the first place was to make sure that he wasn't mentioned in them.

Stone resumed. "Like Vronsky said, you two weren't given the riches. What could you do with your feeble upbringing? What could you aspire to without dough? All you could do was go to sleep on muck dreams and takeout fast food glory, hoping, maybe, by chance, of something greater.

"And here's the brainteaser. This is what I've been stuck up on." The next moment was one of rare candour for Stone. To the audience, his concise verbal marathons were the main event, but they had never heard Stone speak so purposefully of himself. "Truthfully, your problem, Baxter, is *the* problem, *the* puzzle, *the* mathematical X, that I've been grappling with my entire life in law.

"The question is where does your chain of misery end? How do I unlock the centuries-old ball from around your ankle and emancipate your worthless ass to give it some value? How do the masses view the problem? They chant words like "*Society!*" "*Education!*" "*Television!*" And I sang with them. Yes, I thought that was the right song too. But now, here, today, I can finally say poddle-cock to that tune. I shout a high-heaven no. Can I hear a high heaven?" He looked out at the audience. "Well?"

"High heaven," they said quietly.

"No," said Stone.

"High heaven," they said louder.

"No."

"*High heaven!*" they shouted.

"*No!*" Stone shouted back.

He held his hands up for them to stop. "Here's the real answer, ladies and gentlemen. Here's the embodiment of all that ails us. Here before us is the point of rot that spreads out and blankets all our good."

Judge Stone pointed out into the audience. He set his manicured nail hovering between the eyes of Mrs. Baxter. "I say that that woman over there. That mother.

Yes, you, Mrs. Baxter. Please, if you wouldn't mind standing up." Mrs. Baxter obliged. "Feast your eyes, folks. Here stands a woman who trudged through the snow and sleet for...what was it...for...."

Stone cuffed the back of Marchie's head.

"Four days," responded Marchie.

"Four heartbreaking days. Oh, how awful this must have been for you, Mrs. Baxter, sitting through the goop of your boy's foul-ups. How dedicated you were to sit here, with your quivering lips and your eyes running. And the topper, to be Baxter's only character reference. Not one liver-lipped soul but yourself would speak up for him. But when your time came, that didn't stop you from making a beautiful, ignorant, almost utterly incoherent speech. Such a rambling speech about how lovely, how good, how one chance more, your son is. I mean, my God, Baxter, do you actually care for this woman?"

"Yes, Judge. I do."

"And why didn't you ask anyone else to speak for you? Is there something subliminal in all this? Was your mother brought here as a flashing bulb? Is she the lesson I needed to learn? Baxter, are you running this class?"

"Judge Stone," interrupted Vronsky, "can you be asking all these questions? You're like throwing...see, my whole procedural game's being revealed here."

"Vronsky as if you've ever answered, or known an an-

- 103 -

swer, as delicate as Mrs. Baxter. So, Son Baxter, do you know the answer? Are you my master and I your pupil?"

"I asked my mum because I knew she'd be honest."

"Really? That's the reason? That's all? Is he right, Mrs. Baxter? Are you, as Son Baxter said...are you honest?"

"Please, Mr. Stone. He's a good boy," said Mrs. Baxter. "He just shammed up with the wrong crowd."

"Listen to her, Baxter. This woman is standing up for you even when she's in my crosshairs. Mrs. Baxter, don't you see what you've done? No, never mind. Don't answer that. You don't have the X-ray vision that I have. How could you see that you're part of the chain? I'm the one who has to open the blinds. I'm the one who has to turn on my soldering iron and crack time's curse. You're the one.... Sorry, did you say Baxter got with the wrong crowd? Do you know how many mothers have said that before? And how easy I was to dismiss them. My mistake entirely. Because you've all been right. There has been a wrong crowd. And you've been its leaders, Mrs. Baxter. You mothers.

"Son Baxter, come here."

Julian took a step toward Stone. Stone waved him closer. When Julian was in kicking distance, Marchie swung his foot out and kicked Julian in the side of the ribs. Marchie always administered the contact justice. Stone felt physical humiliation was essential when the people who caused it were of similar classes. Also,

Stone had a deep fear of human contact and the contagion gifts that went along with it.

"How's that feel, Baxter?" asked Stone. "That's your first lesson in hurt. Obviously, no one had the guts to teach you that before. Now, look at that woman." Stone pointed at Julian's mother. "See her? That woman struggled for you. She believed in you. Wept for you. Probably even prayed for you. How admirable of her, eh? I said how admirable of her."

There were murmurs of agreement from the court. Vronsky said, "You've never been righter, Judge Stone."

"You know what I have to say about Mrs. Baxter?" asked Stone. "About her impassioned love for her son? How beautiful, right? Mommy loves you, Julian. Mommy's big, bright, bouncy boy. Mommy thinks you're going to be the bestest everest." Stone chuckled lightly. Under his breath, he said, "Bestest everest," and this really got him started. He leaned toward Julian and laughed in his face. This made Stone laugh harder.

The court stayed silent. Vronsky stood attentively, looking for an opening to include himself with Stone's laughter. Stone gasped. He cried. He waved Marchie over. Marchie held the silver plate up to Stone's chin while Stone dribbled and spit into it. As he brushed the tears and run-off phlegm from his face, Stone waved his personal guards toward Mrs. Baxter.

The two guards who closed in on Mrs. Baxter were

the rock-hards[6] that Stone asked for. They slapped their bats in their open palms, happy to finally be given something to do. Happy not to have to sit around sweating through their uniforms (which were jogging pants and tank tops). Here was a head to bounce (if necessary, if the person in question instigated). As each guard grabbed Mrs. Baxter roughly by the shoulder, Julian said, "My mum had nothing to do with this."

"Yes she did," said Stone. "And now she's outta here. The lady you can't live without. Your rock. I'm booting her full time. Don't fret, Master Baxter, I'm not throwing her in the Big House. I'm not that cruel. But I am freeing you. I'm giving you your life for the first time in your life. From here on out, Mrs. Baxter is *person non gratis* in our humble city. Pack your bags, Momma. You're done in this old shambling town."

Julian ran at the guards. One of them swung his bat at him.

"Don't worry, Jules. Mum forgives you," said Mrs. Baxter.

---

6 The guards were part of another lawsuit Stone had won mid-career. His contention was that the type of uniform guard that applied for court bailiff did so because they thought it was a light-stress occupation. That person knew nothing of hand-to-hand combat. That guard stood around looking superior because of the uniform, the dusty Gatt, the knowledge that he/she wasn't being sent down river. "I don't want some museum watcher," Stone told the courts. "Give me burly hardbodies. Give me men brandishing ball bats. Men who still have other men's flesh under their nails. I want my posse to be the arms and legs of me. I want men who will mirror Stone-Time."

Then one of the guards pushed her hard through the swinging door marked JAIL, leaving Julian, arms dangling uselessly at his sides, to watch it swing shut behind her.

Stone's court was located amongst the low-ends, the people, the jobs, that breathed on the get-by. Julian followed Vronsky through these streets, completely unaware of the half-empty shopping malls, the used car and bicycle lots, artists studios, flop houses, chain food stores, and do-it-yourself law firms. Vronsky was taking them to a diner to wait out the appeals verdict, which he had appealed for by using a series of stomps and hand movements. Marchie had nodded that he understood and then whispered to Stone, who gave Vronsky the thumbs up in return. Appeals took anywhere from one minute to three months, but if a lawyer didn't appeal immediately, the right was nullified.

They stepped into Stealy Anne's Family Eats Diner. Stealy Anne's had a tie-in with Stone's court that offered the meal discount to any and all patrons who went to see Stone. All an eater had to do was show their Stone stub and they were given the eater's discount of either fifteen percent (for Bringers) or twenty-five percent (for Pewers). Families were given the golden discount of twenty-five percent for being part of the extended Stone family. All they needed were birth certificates, baby photos, or strong resemblances to their mums and dads.

"How'd you do, Vronsky?" asked the hostess.

"I got one, Chili Dean," said Vronsky.

"That's a first," said Chili Dean.

Chili Dean stood behind a chipped wood-stained podium with a handwritten paper sign taped to it that read: FAMILIES SAY HI FIRST. "Counter's free," she said, tipping her pink papier-mâché king's crown as they passed by her. "And remember to eat them eats, gentlemen," she said.

"And same to you," said Vronsky.

To get to the counter, they walked through the two inches of water that covered most of the restaurant's floor. Stealy Anne's, like many of the downtown stores, had a water runoff problem. This was partly the fault of the heavy Metraville snowfalls and the absence of any snow removal program (the program was cancelled years ago so that Metraville could keep its public pools open during the summer). The other part of the problem was heavy rainfalls during the spring and summer. Add to this the cut-rate drainage and sewer systems and Metraville's water problems began to fill up.[7]

---

7 Many of the stores were now taking advantage of the water deposit program at the Lanigan's Chain of Banks. Lanigan's had a banking concept that the city's most popular and rich entrepreneur, Dash Lanigan, had grabbed onto: "We're going to take that rusty bank clunker and restart it full speed" (Dash's words). Lanigan's was a financial kingdom, but the bank's biggest draw was that they also accepted water by the barrel, for which they paid

"What did you mean you got one?" Julian asked Vronsky.

"Got one what?" asked Vronsky. "Strawberry pancakes? That sounds delicious."

"Not the pancakes. You told that girl when we came in that you got one."

"You mean Chili Dean? Sure, I told her I got one. Got one. Yeah, I got one. You should have seen me in court."

"I was there."

"Oh, yeah. Baxter. Sorry, man. I thought you went to the washroom."

"But I don't understand. How'd you get one in court?"

"What you mean? Look at you. You're a free man. To me, that's a result."

"Vronsky, I lost my mum."

"Yeah, okay. You lost your mum. I know. That's not the result you were expecting. But, see, Stone's a heavy hitter. You got to witness a guy who likes to punish a person uniquely. Stone actually comes through on his desire. Just throwing some guy in the slammer for a spell, or handing out suspended time, community serv-

---

their customers forty bits a deposit. There were plans afoot to start paying for certain woods, armories, and glass. So, at a place like Stealy Anne's, one employee—in this case, Chili Dean—would be assigned the mop-up job. This would entail mopping up then ringing out the water into one of several barrels that was kept in the back room.

ice, that doesn't sit well with him. He wants to push law's potential.

"Like how is sending a pickpocket up to Peace Island going to change a person? That guy's not likely coming back more informed. Stone's philosophy is to ban the guy from wearing shoes. That'll alter the jailbird's perception of himself without pushing the slammer as part of the equation. Stone thinks that'll turn the guy into a good-standing member. Though, the way he lighted up today with this mum trip...we may have witnessed a new plateau in Stone Law."

"My mother's not a criminal."

"Brother, that's so far off the issue."

The waiter behind the counter interrupted them. "What can I get you, boys?"

"We want your Berry-Merry Mix-Up Pancakes," said Vronsky.

Julian grabbed Vronsky by the shirt collar. "We're talking about my mum."

"Hear that, Mama Dean," Chili Dean said to the woman behind the counter. "The boys are fighting over their mama."

"I see it, Chili Dean. Like I told you, that's one thing you never had to worry about being an only child."

"We're not talking about our mum," said Julian. "We're talking about my mum. Vronsky lost her today."

"You lost your mama?" asked Chili Dean.

"Well, not really. She got...see, I was...I got involved in something I shouldn't...Judge Stone decided...." Julian didn't know how to explain.

"Well, if Judge Stone decided something, he must know what he's doing," said Mama Dean.

"That's what I'm telling him, Mama Dean," said Vronsky. "Can we get coffee too?"

Julian watched Mama Dean pour their coffees. Like Chili Dean, Mama Dean wore a brown-coloured dress with a yellow tie. The sleeves of her dress were long on her arms, and she pulled the cuff over her palm before taking the handle of the coffee pot.

Mama Dean put the coffees in front of "the boys." Vronsky was busy wiping his jacket collar where Baxter had grabbed him. Vronsky wasn't mad at Julian about grabbing him. All his clients got restless, maybe a little personal, after sentencing. But why'd they always have to fingerprint his suits? He'd had those woolly fabrics crafted custom. He thought a baggy suit made him look more formidable to his clients, the forehead-frowning juries, and all those stern-faced judges. Vronsky's suit revealed the advocut[8] he knew was buried inside him. The problem that Vronsky missed

---

8 Advocut was a Vronsky coinage—part of a fantasy tele-video ad that he worked and reworked in his mind that finished with the tag line, "Because it's my job to cut the competition in half." As he said this, he swung a machete through a cardboard cutout of a man in a suit.

– 111 –

about the suits was that every time he walked into court, every time he paced in front of the jury and judge, his suit swung close to his bony frame, undoing any menace he hoped to convey.

On one occasion, Vronsky had forgotten to tighten his belt (the waist being made five sizes bigger by request) and as he shuffled around the court, his pants fell around his ankles. He pretended nothing happened, turning his walk into a waddle, but Stone, who was presiding, said, "Son, are you shooting a junk party into your system?" Vronsky was especially proud of this anecdote. He had told it to Julian so many times that he didn't even need to start at the beginning.

"To what I said, 'Your Honour, I'd look less strung out if any of my clients ever paid me.' And even Stone thought that was funny. And that's one of the cases I actually almost won," Vronsky said as he looked at Julian for approval.

"Are you trying to get money out of me?" asked Julian.

"Why would I be telling you otherwise?"

"But you didn't win my case."

"Let's not start breaking down the word *win*. We'll just get bogged down in mazes. As we sit here, I'm already stuck in several semantic conjungles with my former clients over the same issue."

"Vronsky, you lost my mum."

"Come on, Baxter. You got to stop saying that. She

lost herself. A witness like her saying what she was saying.... I'm not saying she deserved the big city boot. I don't know all the facts of her case. I just know from what I've been hearing, and I know what I'm about to say is harsh and I don't mean any disrespect to your mum, but word is she got what was coming to her."

"You're the one who told her to stand up and say all that stuff."

"No way you're pinning this on me. Yes, I told her to say a couple of nice things about her boy. Excuse me, I meant you, Baxter, you. But obviously, when I told her to say something, I didn't mean for her to choose the words she did. And when it comes down to it, what really sunk her were all those crazy inflections of hers. I tried to object and overrule her as much as I could, but she just wasn't listening to me."

"So, it's my mum's fault that she's going to jail?"

"She's been kicked out of the city. She's not going to jail. That's a key point right there."

"But she shouldn't have been in a position to get exiled in the first place."

"I totally agree with you. It should have been you. I kept telling Stone, 'Get rid of the kid. Kick her boy out.'"

"Can we do that? Can I take her place?"

"We've done all we could. The appeal's been rejected. What's left? I dunno."

"The appeal? When did that get rejected?"

"Two minutes ago? Maybe ten?"

"What? I didn't know this."

"I wanted to finish my breakfast before we got talking over the appeal."

"But how did you find out?"

"Tiny told me." Vronsky pointed to the short-order cook behind the counter, who snapped a finger pistol at them. "He took the call."

"So that's it? There's nothing that can change Stone's mind?"

"Not that I know. Mama Dean, we're going to need more coffee."

Julian turned his stool away from Vronsky. He was just in time to see his mum stumble by the restaurant window. She waved to him. One of the security guards saw her do this and pushed her in the back with the baseball bat that he held between his hands. She looked tired. Her back more hunched. Her grey hair a bit greyer than the day before. Julian grabbed Vronsky's arm. "There she is. Come on, help me."

"What?" Vronsky asked through a mouthful of berries and pancake.

"Those cops are dragging her away."

Vronsky checked his watch. "Yeah, that seems about right. They let her pack a couple of bits. Now she's back to the courthouse for her big vamoose." Vronsky noticed Julian hadn't touched his food yet. He wanted the second meal but wasn't sure how Baxter would react if he asked for it. He guessed it best to start slow: "Can I have your garnish?"

Julian pushed the plate at Vronsky as he ran to the door. He would have been able to catch up to his mum if he hadn't gotten tangled up in the doorway with Judge Stone and Marchie, who had just entered the restaurant. Judge Stone pointed at Julian and said, "Apprehend that man until I sit down."

Marchie grabbed Julian by the waist. Judge Stone skirted around them, making sure not to touch them.

"Judge Stone, save my mum," said Julian.

"What'd he say?" Stone asked Chili Dean.

"Something about his momma needing helping."

"A mother? I've had enough of those types for a few days."

Stone made his way to his table. Julian continued to call out to him, but even if he'd stayed put, Stone would never have been able to hear Julian over Marchie's laboured breathing.

"Let me go," said Julian.

"I...can't...until...Mr...Stone...says...."

Chili Dean came to the front to see what the fuss was about. "Man, what you say about your momma?"

"Maybe you can help. My mum's leaving. I don't want her to go."

"Nobody wants to see their momma go."

"But I can stop it."

"What's going on out there?" called a man through the service window.

"Papa Dean, man out here by himself, not saying bye to his momma."

"He's by himself, that's why."

"No. She's off and leaving."

"She's off and going? But what about family?" Papa Dean asked.

"Papa Dean, why you asking about family?" asked Mama Dean.

Judge Stone interrupted them. He yelled from his seat, "Marchie, where are my frites?"

Marchie, who was resting on the ground, pulled himself up and hobbled toward the dining area.

"Family?" asked Chili Dean.

"Family," sputtered Marchie.

"*Family!*" shouted Mama Dean.

"But where's that fella's?" said Papa Dean.

Julian had begun walking to the section cordoned off for Judge Stone. "I don't want my mum to go. Not like this."

"Mama Dean, man's causing a fuss," called Chili Dean.

"Papa Dean," cried Mama Dean.

Papa Dean burst out of the kitchen's swinging door, wearing a brown suit, yellow tie, and a yellow visor cap. He brandished a mop in his hands. "Ruckus?" he said. He pointed the dripping mop end at Julian. "This is family owned. We don't have time for no onesies like yourself causing a ruckus. Now inch your way outwards before I have to clean your face off."

Julian backed out slowly. Chili Dean held the door for him. "Thanks for arriving," she said as Julian stepped outside.

*

Julian wanted to take some action. To do something decisive. He headed to Stone's court, to where the action was. Exactly, he thought, *was* was the right word. My actions are past-due. Whatever the actions could have been, they've expired now. He wanted to save his mum. But even that word—*save*—even that word was beginning to lose its force for him.

He stopped at a street corner to figure out where to go next. Near the corner, a Meat Man stood behind his open barbeque. A cardboard sign was taped to one of the barbeque legs: MAKE ENDS MEAT: MEAT – $2, MEAT + LIQUID – $3. A veteran Meat Man customer never asked questions. No one ever said, "You got any chicken?" Maybe the Meat Man had some chicken. Maybe he was serving pork. Might have been lean beef. Or even a mash-up of all three plus other less familiar flesh. But the Meat Man was never telling, and a choosy customer should never ask because, as all Meat Man customers knew, once spoken, then owned.

The Meat Man waved at Julian and then speared a slab of uncooked meat out of his bucket, dripping brown juice all over his deeply smudged apron. Julian shook his head no. Any sound at all was a tacit yes to a Meat Man. They even tried to coax a noise from their prey, as this Meat Man tried with Julian. "That's you, Chops," the Meat Man said, pointing at the dripping hunk of meat.

Julian kept shaking his head. Traffic zipped by without any opening for escape. The Meat Man threw the severed chunk onto the open fire. "Eh, Chops. Your meat is getting cooked so fine. You'll be done in a minute, Chops. Done and ready to be shipped off, Chops. Eh, Chops? Eh?"

Julian tried stepping out onto the road. A car had to stop quickly. The driver stuck his head out of his glassless window and yelled, "Useless loafgroper!"

The Meat Man looked at the driver. The driver looked at the Meat Man. The driver tried peeling away, but his car stalled. The Meat Man launched himself at the driver, opening the passenger-side door, and flipping the charred meat into the driver's lap, then yelled, "Take Chops' unwanted food. Eat Chops' food. Eat Chops."

Julian took the break in traffic to skirt his way across the street. Midway down the block, he ran down an alley and came out onto another, almost identical, street. The street was lined on both sides with storefronts, the odd one still in business. A guy stood in front of one of the empty stores beside a yellow wheelless wagon that had the red words INKY'S BEAT written across the side. Julian recognized the guy as a Syndicate member named Inky who sold stolen newspapers out of his wagon. Julian was happy to see someone familiar.

"How do I get to Stone's court?" Julian asked.

"I'm no bad guy," said Inky.[9]

"Sorry," Julian said. "I thought you were Syndicate."

"You Narco?" asked Inky.

"No."[10]

"I'm Syndicate," said Inky.

"Me too. I'm Baxter."

"Me Inky. Stone's is that way," Inky said, pointing off down the street. "A couple of rights. A couple of lefts. But just keep going that way. I got to go there my-

---

9 A Syndicate rule was that an employee never thought of himself or herself as part of any illegal element. New employees were always asked, "Have you ever been sacked by a cop?" If the answer was no, then the Syndicate said, "See, you aren't a petty thief, so quit thinking you are. You're like everyone else. You're an employee doing a job. Making a couple of bucks off the backs of others. That's just business." Now, if the answer was yes, "Yes, I've been arrested," well, the solution was easy. The Syndicate didn't shut their door on someone who had gone down to the Big House for a spell. They didn't just kiss off someone who was considered a two-bit by the rest of society. What sense would there be in losing a potential can of experience? No, the guy, the gal, who says during round-the-room introductions at a Syndicate hiring convention that, yeah, they've got crook pasts, then the massaged Syndicate answer was that no they don't have crook pasts; that's part of their work experience.

10 Metraville law states that any undercover cop who asks a potential perp if they're Syndicate must respond in kind if the perp asks.

self in a few days. I'm going to see if I can get my wheels back from Stone. What'd he get from you?"

"My mum."

Inky threw one of his papers at Julian. "That you?"

There was a picture of Julian on the front of the *Metraville Stars*. The shot must have been taken as he and Vronsky were coming out of the courthouse. In the photo, Julian was wide-eyed, staring beyond the camera, Vronsky beside him, Vronsky's hands clenched in victory. The caption underneath:

HARD TIME MOMMA

Julian began reading the article:

For the first time, a mother goes down. A lowlife, Baxter, saw his mother incarcerated on his behalf today. The Honourable Judge Stone sent the lady down to crack rocks as an example to bad parents everywhere. Baxter's former employer, a Mr. Shandy, who asked to be on record, has this to say: "Baxter's mum, she was everywhere causing mayhem. The streets will be safer without her."

"You skim, you buy," interrupted Inky.

"But they're writing lies about me."

"That's their right. Nothing to do with me. Now come on, pay the piper."

"I've got no money."

Inky grabbed the paper out of Julian's hands. "Get out of my face before I have you done for unsolicited reading."

"I just want to see—"

"Exactly. That's the whole reason we're barking. Because you just want a little see. Why should you see for free while another guy has to see for cash? See what I'm getting at, mummy's boy?"

"Hey, Stone could have taken your mum."

"Stoney would never touch my mum."

"How do you know?"

"Because my mum would never get herself tied up with a son like you."

"But you're in the Syndicate just like me."

"And my mum hasn't spoken to me since."

Inky was talking so much that he was practically giving away the news for free. He decided to move on, to find himself a street that wasn't so dead. He picked up his wagon and, with some difficulty, rested it on his chest and wobbled off, cursing the weight of his job and cursing Baxter for reminding him how long it'd been since he'd talked with his mother.

Julian walked the opposite way from Inky. Not two

blocks later, a couple of kids came toward him from the other direction. These were a couple of Syndicate kids. Julian could tell from the way their pants were tied to their ankles.[11]

The kids coming toward Julian began rubbing their eyes as they pretended to cry. "I want my mummy," said one of them.

"Mummy," said the other kid.

"What do you two want?" asked Julian.

"Mummy? Where are you, Mummy?"

Julian tried to push past the kids.

"Watch it, Mummy," one of them said.

"Was that Mummy?" said the other kid.

"Mummy," said the first kid.

Trying to reason with them, Julian said, "How would you feel if you lost your mums?"

"What happened to my mum?" asked the first kid.

"Is my mum sick?" asked the other.

"No, nothing's wrong with your mums. But see

---

11 Syndicate kids were exclusively hired to go after the BUDGE products that the MAZE-A-FIX-INC Company had built. These were cars, safes, store locks, the you-name-its of the security world. MAZE-A-FIX bragged (well, used to brag) about its unique brand of customer-specific custom-molded tiny tools without which the MAZE-A-FIX products couldn't work. What the company had failed to anticipate—what countless tests, surveys, research groups had blindly overlooked—was that any small child or little person, without the aid of the BUDGE tools could infiltrate any MAZE-A-FIX product. The MAZE-A-FIX marketing branch collectively smacked their heads over the one demographic they'd dismissed as being irrelevant MAZE-A-FIX consumers.

how worried you were. Now you know how I feel."

The boys started crying. Sputtering at first, the crying revved up as the kids realized the full horror of losing their mums.

"Jesus, calm down. Your mums haven't gone anywhere."

People passing along the street stopped to watch the commotion. A woman who had been pushing a baby carriage said, "What did you do to these children?"

"Nothing!" Julian said.

"Mummy," sobbed one kid.

"Mummy," answered the other one.

"Are you the father?" asked the woman.

"I'm not a dad," said Julian.

"Come here, sweeties. Come on. We'll get you home."

The kids ran into the woman's open arms. They rubbed the tears from their eyes. When they had calmed down, they began moving through the crowd, pickpocketing everyone within reach, slipping their loot into the baby carriage. One of the children noticed Julian watching them. "Move along, Mummy," the kid told him.

"Yeah, Mummy," shouted one of the crowd.

"No one wants Mummy," said the other kid.

"Mummy! Mummy!" the group yelled.

Julian gave up. He ran down the block. He ran

down another alley. He ran down another street. Even this far away, he could still hear the Mummy chant ringing in the air. Mummy. The papers had nailed him. But the Syndicate and the public were the ones who were running with it. That word. *Mummy*. A person could make that word so hateful. Add a pinch of whine, a dash of shriek to that name and then watch people's shoulders tense and their nails begin to dig into their palms. Their eyes would search the restaurant, the shopping mall, the bus stop. People would wonder whose kid was saying that word *Mummy*. People wouldn't blame the children either, just the mum. They would blame the mum who taught her kid that tone of voice. MUMmy mumMY mUMMy. There it is again, people would think. Who was that Mummy? And the answer, always the answer now, the sap people's eyes and minds would set upon would be Julian. He was Mummy.

A few blocks later, Julian was able to see the courthouse looming in the distance. Well, the courthouse itself didn't loom. What stood out, flapping hard in the wind, was the oversized flag with Stone's face on both sides, attached to a twenty-five-foot flagpole. That flag was a beacon, drawing all from far and wide to come see Stone Justice.

There was a man bouncing a ball against the side of the court's brick wall when Julian got there. The man caught the ball and waved at Julian. "Hey, Baxter."

"Hey," Julian said. He was more concerned with the giant CLOSED sign that covered the front doors.

"Baxter, it's me, Tugs."

"Oh. Hey, Mr. Shandy."

"What's going on? Why you here? Why haven't you hightailed it away from the law?"

"I'm here to get my mum."

"Don't you get the picture, Baxter?"

"How do you mean?"

"Baxter, you're fired. I can't have a guy like you working for me. You're sick with backward-thinking poison."

"But I've been trying to quit the Syndicate—"

"Trying. God, Baxter, you should have left months ago. That's not even the point. You spectacularly lack all the qualities that my new theories embody. You were a real test for me. I'm sure I've learned something quite valuable from you. I just know I have."[12]

"Which reminds me," Tugs told Julian. "I want

---

12 Tugs Shandy's theories. This was what set a manager like Tugs apart from all the other mid-level bosses. He prided himself on being on the ground floor of new crime, where crime was getting re-evaluated and redefined. Let a judge such as Stone try his hand at transforming law; let's see what he could come up with. Tugs would be up late with his bubbling beakers, mixing and concocting his own transformative crime. And Tugs' solution to crime, when he found it, wouldn't resemble anything like what the population thought of as old crime. Old Crime made people feel bad. Old Crime swung baseball bats and fingered guns errantly. Old Crime was like the kind a person found lurking in the shadows of alleyways, wearing long coats, talking menacingly low about

"fucking shit up." Tugs shuddered at the very baseness of such talk. He was plotting the end of mean, fearful, evil crime.

He was going to usher in a New Look Crime, crime that worked with the community to make everyone feel better about being robbed. And sure, Tugs' focus was on the burglar aspects of crime right now because the department he headed in the Syndicate was the burglary division. Let him re-invent robbery first; let him prove to his brethren that change was possible. Then he could pounce on the other crimes. All those murdering body-damaging embezzlers that sullied the look of crime and, by association, the Syndicate itself.

What Tugs wanted from his employees was to have their crimes out in the open, not hidden under subterfuge, like Old Crime. That's why Tugs did all his business out in the street. He didn't hide inside the alley; he hung out at the mouth of the alley, so he could be seen. Not for himself. Not so he could have a handful of witnesses who'd be able to stand up in court and say they saw Tugs at such and such a place and such and such a time rather than in some convenience store on Main with his hand in the till. No, he wanted people to see Tugs. To put Tugs' face to crime, a face they could say yes to when they thought of thieving.

Within the Syndicate, Tugs was considered a maverick. The kind of freethinking criminal that could really push the company to new heights of prosperity. Could being the operative word. Because Tugs' coworkers, sure they saw the potential behind Tugs' new crime, but saw and enacted, well, that was a grey area for the crews. They liked the idea of having more effective ways of carrying out crime, but when they were put in criminal situations, faced with a bag of stolen loot and a bunch of cop sirens blaring close by, on came the nylon stocking mask, hunched went the body, and back swung the motions of Old Criminal ways. Even the cops, who begrudgingly approved of Tugs' new approaches to criminality, even they fell back on the same police patter when they confronted him about a case they were trying to crack. "Shandy," the cops would say, "we know you're trying to make a difference here, but we're still going to have to beat your ass a little to get answers from you." Of course, the big change was that they did this at the front of the alley, and only after they'd asked Tugs if he was having a good day and if he could spare a minute (the your velvet sack[13] back."

"I don't know where mine is. I think the cops took it."

"Then you're going to have to reimburse me from this." Tugs handed Julian an envelope. On the front was written: FOR JULIAN'S MA. "Just a little something that me and the guys put together. We figured your mother would need some seed money to start herself up again. I mean, we didn't know her, but we appreciated the way she stuck it to Stone."

"She got mixed up with Stone because of me."

"You sure did let her down." Tugs had been fiddling with a pack of matches. He absentmindedly tried putting them in the pocket of his purple dress pants, forgetting that he had no pockets. The matches fell to the ground. He bent down and picked them up. "You should have thrown yourself at Stone. You should have said, 'Take me. Don't take her. Please, don't take my mum away.'"

Julian asked hopefully, "Do you think that would have helped?"

"That's not the point. People want to see you fight for them. They want you to go the distance."

"But when it was happening, I didn't know what

difference being that these were sentiments they actually meant now).

13 Shandy's velvet sacks were his trademark within the ranks of the Syndicate. His men got them when they started and were expected to use them on all their assignments.

to do."

"You don't have to remind me. I saw it." Tugs took the envelope from Julian's hand. "The little gestures mean the utmost." He ripped open the envelope and took some of the money out. "Now I'm taking this for the sack. You still owe the till fifty." Without thinking, Tugs tried putting the bills into the breast pocket of his purple jacket. The bills fluttered out over the ground. "Jeez, Baxter. Help me with these."

As they squatted down to pick up the money, Tugs leaned in close to Julian and began whispering, trying to create a conspiratorial bond between the two of them. "Baxter, the crew gets what you're going through. We've all had to deal with Stone Justice at one time or another in our lives. And we know how it can stick to you.

"I mean, look at the two of us right now. We're down in the mud and puddles because of how Stone busted my guts way back when. I showed up in his courthouse, I stood before him, and he saw right into me. He flew past those layers of clever guy, past my talents as a decent pickpocket, added two plus two, and Stone isolated four. And that's how he caught me. His massive hands grabbed ahold of me and started ripping. Front pocket, back pockets, coat pockets. Then he smacked me with a ten-year ban on owning even one pocket. Not a single one for the full stretch.

"At the time, though, does he say anything about my backpacks and purses? No, of course not. But my mind has already gone there. Because if you throw a hole in front of me hoping that I'm going to fall in, I'm going to find a way to leap over it. That is, until Stone gets wind of my scheme, and out come two plus two again. And how does he catch on? Do I get caught using a bag? Does someone squeal on me? No. Stone just knows. Stone and Marchie show up at my house one night. Marchie knocks on my door. I answer it. Stone shakes his head at me. Marchie does all the asking. I hand over all my carry items because I know when my goose is glazed.

"Now, the problem with you, Baxter, is that you're both a crap thief and Stone-Punched. I have expertise and leadership skills. You, you're lacking on all sorts of fronts. Like for instance, how much were you pulling in a month working for me?"

"I wasn't making anything."

"You're telling me that after you paid your Syndicate fees you made nothing?"

Julian had actually been borrowing money from his mother to pay his fees. He told her the money was for groceries. Though he didn't tell Tugs this. "I was paying my fees out of my own pocket."

"Are you mocking me with that word?" Tugs asked.

"What're you talking about?"

"How could you use that word *pocket* with all I'm going through. You can't be nonchalant about a thing like pockets. Trust me. Once they're gone, you realize they were your first love. Imagine trying to warm your hands unrequited." Tugs looked at his bare hands. Caressed them with his eyes. Spoke to them, "Alright. Forget it. I got carried away. Stone forgiven. Stone forgotten." He looked back at Julian. "This fees business. You're, in a way, saying that I robbed from you. In a sense I mean."

"You didn't steal from me."

"Sort of. Think about it. Like you paid me for a job you didn't do. I was getting your dough for no reason."

"I was paying the company its fees."

"Lay off the fees. Forget about them. I'm talking about me. I'm talking about clearance records here. See, Baxter, numbers matter. At the end of the day, my bosses are wondering, is Tugs Shandy hitting his targets? As team leader, I got to make sure my division brings in its numbers. And if I don't, my bosses are going to wonder, is Tugs Shandy pushing his people or is he letting them go through the motions? Should we find some guy—some guy who's younger who will work for less? But they won't even think about Junior if I can smack your dough on my pile. Bosses start seeing Tugs Shandy as a moneymaker. And if Tugs Shandy pushes himself, they'll think Tugs Shandy must be pushing his men. Because the truth is, I'm not pulling my weight. I need better numbers. And technically, your dough, I mean the dough you didn't make, that's not a job well done on your part."

"Tugs, I don't care. I just want to see my mum."

"So, your money is my theft?"

"If you tell me where my mum is."

"Perfect. She's around the corner."

"What?"

"Yeah. That's where the buses pick up the criminals."

As Julian started to get up, Tugs grabbed him by the wrist. "Let go. I've got to try something to save her," said Julian.

"I want the rest of the money in the envelope. I'm going to add that to my earnings."

Julian held it out to Tugs. "Take it then."

"Couldn't you put up a fight? Say, 'Stop, thief!'"

Julian dropped the envelope into Tugs' lap. Tugs stood up and pushed Julian to the ground. "See you later, Mummy." Then he took off, dribbling his tennis ball against the ground as he ran away.

Julian got up and ran around the corner of Stone's courthouse. There were large crowds, partitioned behind ropes, and an array of Stone Men, ball bats in hand. Julian cupped his hand over his eyes, hoping this would guide him to his mum. There was no sign of his five-foot-three mum, in her long grey coat, with her curly, faded, dyed black hair, sitting quietly trying not to take up too much room. Trying, as she always tried, not to get in anyone's way. No mum of Julian's waiting at any of the loading bays for her last trip out of town.

One of Stone's guards, one Julian recognized from his court case, passed by. "Excuse me," Julian said.

The guard turned to look down at Julian's hand on his shoulder. "You get off me, okay?" he said.

"I'm sorry. I'm looking for my mother."

"Yeah, so?"

"Are you here with her?"

The guard grabbed Julian by the scruff. He marched him to another guard who stood watch over a pack of women. This second guard held a baseball bat between his hands, which he pushed at the women when he had the urge.

"I'm looking for this boy's mother," said the first guard. All the women looked up hopefully.

"Her name's May. May Baxter," said Julian

"We got a May Baxter?"

"I'm here," said May.

"Show your face then," said the guard holding Julian.

The group parted. May stepped out from the middle. "Here I am," she said. "Oh, look, everyone," May said to the group, "here's my son. Hello! Hello, son."

The group waved. Someone said, "He's a cute one, May." Another said, "Such a good boy to come and say goodbye to his mother." They all agreed.

"Walter, may I see my son?" May asked the guard

covering her.

Walter didn't want to take responsibility for her question. He looked at the other guard, who just shrugged. May took this as a yes. The guard holding Julian pushed him toward May but didn't let go of Julian's scruff. May took hold of her son's hand.

"Where are they taking you?" Julian asked.

"It's very exciting. We're headed out east. All the ladies are going to rent a house together. And we're going to work odd jobs."

A bus pulled up to the curb in front of them. The bus door hissed open. The driver eased himself out of his seat and walked to the bottom step. "Let's get this over with," he said.

One of the guards handed the driver a piece of paper and a wad of cash. The driver nodded. "They put their own bags on."

"You heard the man. Get your stuff on. And let's move it," the guard said.

"I'll write when I have an address," said May.

"I'll call you," said Julian.

"You finally got a phone?"

"I'm still working on that."

"Whose are these?" asked the guard pointing toward two aqua-coloured suitcases.

"Oh, those are mine, Dylan," said May.

"Well? You want 'em on the bus or what?"

"On please."

"Okay then, Baxter. Break it up," said Dylan.

"Here I go. Wish me luck," May said to Julian.

There was nothing he could say to stop what was happening. "Good luck."

Dylan pushed May hard in the back. She stumbled forward and fell onto the ground, splitting one of her stockings. As she stood up, she brushed mud and small stones off her clothes and hands.

"Sorry. Just part of the job," he said.

"I understand. You've got your instructions," May said.

The bus started up again. The guard let go of Julian and grabbed Mrs. Baxter by the arm, pulling her up onto the first step of the bus. May waved to Julian as the door hissed shut in her face. He watched her walk down the aisle toward a group of women who had saved her a seat with them.

As she sat down, May looked out at Julian. She waved again at him. Julian waved at her. She waved back. They kept this up until the bus disappeared around the corner and he couldn't see her anymore—though he kept waving a little while longer just in case.

Directive Fork-With (whispers)

His instructions were to follow him. He did.
Mine were to watch him. Eventually he saw
me tailing. This led to a change of plans. He
stopped shadowing his guy; I started peep-
ing on that guy, plus him, and a guy, riding
alone on a tandem bike, who had eyes all
over me. My boss, he always told me, keep
track, keep pace, keep sight. Now my boss,
he said he was also the second guy's boss,
and the third guy's agent. That third one,
he's got a gig disguised as an extra cheese
and mushroom pizza. If I want to lose this
tail, I may have to go to cooking school. But
to do that, I have to give up on him, on the
guy my boss had, on the guy my boss was
working for, and on the girl I was trying to

get with. She's another story. She wanted me. I know she's a front for him, so I wanted her. I suspect her and him of being involved. I don't know how yet. I have no evidence, no documentation, of them together. Brother and sister, I've written in my notes. Maybe father and daughter — I think this because they have the same nose. They have the same eyes. I had a theory going they were the same person, but I slept with him, then her, and I've noted the differences. He was giving, liked to dress up in mother's cloth- ing. She had the lights off, preferred to whisper. When we were finished, she stayed long enough to put on her trench coat, then left by the window. He left by the door. Be- cause of the frustration of them, I've consid- ered getting new instructions, asking for a different case. To do this, I would have to find my boss. He disappeared after I pho- tographed him and his guy delivering furni- ture. I note that they appeared to be trying to cover up something. My boss, now, he's part of the equation. I can't figure out which part. Is he to be undercover, prying his eyes on me? And how to dispose of my notes? I have the varying sized containers. I have X number of pages, that make me W kind of agent. I know these X pages go into Y capsule then are buried MN kilometers away. Are these even the right coordinates? Has my math erred? I've used invisible ink to add them up. Is the ink somehow faulty — am I somehow decoding my notes wrong? Furthermore, my bread and sardine lunches have been scaring the pigeons away. How many more days must I eat noontime meals alone? Or is this how it's supposed to be?

(recorded for training purposes)

"Who'd you say this is?"

"Ken is calling."

"Are you from the hospital?"

"No, sir. I'm calling on behalf of Cruiser Liners with the offer of a luxurious package deal."

"Luxurious. If you only knew how ridiculous that word sounds to me."

"But I've an offer on a service you haven't known before."

"What do you mean? You want to sell me something."

"Yes. Very much."

"Sure. Why not? Everybody else is trying to sell me something. My goddamn doctor just sold me a whole new life. Sorry. You'll have to excuse me, but I'm a lot drunk at the moment. It's how I've been coping."

"Did you say you love vacations?"

"Sure I do. I'd love one right now. Can you give me a vacation from myself?"

"The offer I have is good for two."

"Of course it's for two. Look, buddy, I don't want to dick you around. I can't go anywhere right now. Just to give you an idea...my own mother...she called me a murderer. Can you imagine that?"

"Ken is sorry to hear that."

"Who?"

"Ken."

"Ken?"

"Yes?"

"Ken? Oh, right. You're Ken."

"Hello!"

"Look, I hate to unload on you like this, but would you mind? Can I be honest with you?"

"I'm here to help."

"My doctor...Doctor Rothstein...he's going to...."

"Yes? Sir...?"

"..."

"Sir, did you hang up?"

"Ken...I saw X-rays. You understand? X-rays of myself. I saw them. I saw teeth. There were fingernails. They were growing inside me. I had these headaches... At first, Rothstein, he said they were just headaches...."

"Perhaps if you agree to my terms, all your headaches will disappear?"

"I appreciate what you're trying to do, buddy, but I'm stuck here. I got to get this removed...this cyst.... It's near my coccyx...it's still there. Still thriving on me."

"The trip *is* available for twelve months."

"Oh, I think I get you. You don't mean going on a trip now. You're saying go after the surgery, right?"

"A break from the grindstone. You'd be an odds on favourite to win."

"Yeah, maybe I should play the odds. Look at me. I'm one in a million. Well, two in a million."

"So you would agree to my deal?"

"I don't know. I can't make a decision about anything. Should I be doing this? I was an only child. And now.... Do you come from a big family?"

"I'm only Ken."

"I hear you. Just one. Just like I was. Now here's me and my...sibling. We're the same age. The thing could have been my mum's favourite if it had had the chance."

"I'm offering the chance of a lifetime."

"A lifetime, huh. What? Like me and it grow old together? Like we both pass away on some porch, me sitting on it on a rocking chair?"

"Exactly. A guest and you. Take time to be by yourselves."

"Ah...I can't...I can't keep this.... I can't convince me. Just the thought of.... I'm not doing it."

"Very well. Thank you for the time to hear me out."

"Ken, come on. This isn't easy for me."

"I can call back at a more convenient time?"

"The surgery will be done by then."

"Then have a pleasant good weekend."

"Wait a second...."

"Ken? You still there?"

"Ken?"

"Ken?"[14]

---

14 When was the last time you called a loved one?

FACT

Three percent of the air contained in a person's yawn is poisonous. These poisons are an accumulation of the toxins that a body absorbs during the processes of life. Though rare, a yawn actually wields the power to kill a person. Historians believe that the gesture of covering one's mouth when yawning did not derive as an act of manners, but in fact was done because people feared being tried for murder.

1:12 1:31

Sleepwalker,
arms stretched
ahead of her,
slippers shucking
against pavement,
her sleep cap bent
mid-point, wanders
through knife
fight unscathed.
Three strides away,
falls back to sleep on
the curb, resting
against a parked
car.
November 24

21:23 ● 21:41

Drunks drop
their bottles.
Ended up on
their hands
& knees licking
booze between
broken glass.

September 17

The Slush Times

The bus that rolled on by Julian Baxter was one of those *Wheels-A-Go-Go* company patch-ups that plagued the city at that point. The bus sprayed slush into Julian's face and slid to a stop in the middle of the intersection, idling there, maybe waiting for Baxter, maybe just catching its breath before barrelling through the city some more.

For the *Wheels-A-Go-Go* riders, the guessing, the hoping, the erratic *Go-Go* behaviour was a given. Among themselves, as they waited at the bus stops, riders talked of a past when they could follow a schedule, where going to a stop at a certain time meant that a bus was guaranteed to be there and would stop for the passengers. "Remember when," they all used to say. Now most said, "I heard there was a time when." They'd talk of the past as they ran to catch a *Go-Go* that had barely slowed down near their stop, just as Julian was at that very moment. Julian's expression: one of desperation, a series of downturned facial muscles that all riders hoped to perfect. They believed this expression would positively sway the driver's mood and be the ticket aboard the bus.

For once, Julian was lucky. The bus didn't move. Julian knocked on the doors, and they slowly opened, creaking awake from disuse. The driver, Stanton, looked down at Julian.

"Where you going?" asked Stanton.

"I have no idea," said Julian.

"In an awful hurry for someone going nowhere."

Julian didn't understand what was going on. The *Go-Go* drivers never threw out idle talk. If they opened the doors, the rider was to get on quickly, no eye contact. The best a rider could hope for in the way of chatter was a grunt, nothing more. Questions were out of the question. What did a driver care about a rider? Riders were low-end bumps too out-of-pocket to own their own transportation.

"Are you out of service?" asked Julian.

"*Are you out of service?*" Stanton repeated with an exaggerated whine.

"Pardon?"

"I know your type. If I let you on, you're going to try to provoke me."

"I just want a ride."

"Why?"

"Because I'm tired and cold."

"The heaters are broken on my bus."

"That doesn't matter."

"I like all the windows open."

"The bus will still be warmer than standing out here."

"What's your problem? You running from some kind of trouble?"

"I'm not running from anybody."

Stanton picked up his microphone. He put it to his lips. His voice crackled over the speakers. "Hey, Pokey. What do you think of this gumsack? Good enough for the bottoms of shoes, good enough for here?"

This guy, Pokey, stuck his head out over the top of the stairs. Pokey looked down at Julian. Julian looked up at him. Did Pokey see Julian's soaked jeans and jean jacket? Did Julian see Pokey's unkempt, swirling, brown hair? No. Neither paid any attention to the subtleties, the details, of the other. There was relief on both sides after the once-over. Each to himself, a thank God of he-looks-worse-than-me. A "What happened to that guy?" That wonderful self-reassurance after seeing one of the worse-for-wears that are bumped into in the city.

"He's perfect," said Pokey.

Stanton looked down at Julian. "Turns out I got room for one more."

As Julian climbed up the bus steps, relieved he didn't have to wander the streets aimlessly anymore, Stanton watched Julian's nose. Stanton waited for it.

Then.... Right there. There went Julian's nose. A slight twitch. And another one. Look at this guy, thought Stanton. He's got snow sliding off his head for Christ's sake, and top it off, dressed in soaked pants with dirt on his face. And he still got the nerve to notice the bus smells. Of course the bus smells. How could it not with all those human droppings? All their dandruff. Their sweat. The sneezes, chewed gum, dead skin, dead lice, loose hairs, pimple puss, dried semen, shit flakes, nail clippings, sleep crust. All those little gifts that the riders brought on for each other as they got the most out of their five-buck trip through the city. And this guy was going to blame Stanton for that smell.

"You think I smell, don't you?" said Stanton.

"No I don't. I have a poor sense of smell. I can't smell anything. It runs in my family—on my mum's side," said Julian.

Stanton opened his mouth. "Look in there. Look at my missing teeth. That must mean I'm dirty, right? That must mean de facto that I'm the one who smells? Well the answer to that is that you stink."

Stanton pointed his long, skinny arm out at Julian so Julian couldn't fool himself about who Stanton was talking about. And what could Julian say in return? He knew he smelled off. He knew wandering the streets for days on end wasn't healthy. He'd seen the passersby's stares, the query in their eyes for a guy, underdressed, walking zigzag along streets, sometimes near half asleep. *There* was a directionless guy soaked in who-knows-what. But Julian never held their stares long enough to remember them. Stanton's finger in his face, the fingernail chewed, yellowed, pitted, poking from a glove with the tips cut off—Julian couldn't pretend that someone else, someone Julian was standing near, was going a bit wrong. He was the only one in the lineup this time around. The one who'd been fingered with the stinking crime.

In an attempt to clean himself up, Julian scratched his hand through his hair, sending the rest of the slush down his back, which he tried, almost successfully, to shake out the bottom of his jacket.

A low whining voice called from the back of the bus, "You hear the one about the guy who came in from the cold?"

That voice, that wasn't Pokey's voice. This new guy—the voice was male—this guy was slow and tired, full of gravel, the mouth half closed, the lung air barely escaping.

"No I haven't," replied Pokey to the question.

"Neither did his mortician," said the gravel voice.

Julian kept his eyes on the large yellow bruise on Stanton's chin. He was afraid to look toward the back of the bus where the voices were coming from, afraid even to make eye contact with Stanton. Normal *Go-Go* procedure was to march on the bus, drop change in the money chute, and then hurry as far to the back as possible to get away from the driver. Make the driver forget that you were on the bus, taking up air. But this bus trip already felt different. Thoughts of gross bodily harm punched through Julian's mind. Don't make any contact with anyone, he told himself. Stop mid-bus. Put my head down. Retreat for a spell more.

He dropped a handful of change into the money chute—his last, his only, handful of change, the meticulously counted finder's keepers that he had sought out during his rambles.

Stanton watched the change fall into the chute. He brushed at the wisp of blond hair on the back of his head, and without taking his eyes off the front window, said aloud to everyone on the bus, "You're a dime short there, son."

Julian checked his hands, his jean jacket pockets, and his pant pockets, but found no missing dime. "I must have dropped it outside," he said.

Stanton opened the doors behind Julian. "Why don't you go stand outside until we figure this shortfall out? Do it. Go on. Get out there. I won't drive off."

"You're lying."

"Part of the fun is that you've got to trust me."

Julian's brain was too cold. Days ago, his thoughts settled in mid-thought deep freeze. When Stanton told him to go outside, Julian's chilled reaction was to step out into the snowbank without a fight. He stepped in and sunk right up to his knees.

"Do you want me to go look for it?"

Stanton hadn't thought of this. He'd only gotten as far as the guy standing in the snowbank. "You think you can find it?"

"I could have dropped it anywhere."

"What about finding two empty bottles. They're always lying around. You can use them as a deposit."

Julian looked around. There was a pyramid of snow near the corner that looked about the size of a garbage can. Even if he could melt that snow down, he'd find nothing there. Not on that corner. Same the next. In the part of town they were in, there were only a few garbage cans left. Not standing but toppled, many cut in half. Those garbage cans that had been saved, washed up on the sidewalk, would be kidnapped before long, taken up for scraps by the scavengers.

This wasn't true of all the cans across town—not yet. The mood of the pedestrians, the sense of the city planners, was that garbage cans were obsolete. They just cost too much was the mantra sold to taxpayers. The fact was that the city couldn't find any way to anchor the damn things down any longer. The scavengers were too clever, too needy, too desperate. Frankly, the scavengers were just too damn *too*. And when anything is *too*, the popular thinking went at city hall, well, then, throw that fight. With all the budget cuts the city was having, it'd never be strong enough to beat anybody who was *too*.

The way the city figured it, garbage cans lacked the modern touch. What was the Number-One City doing slumming an idea like past-modern garbage cans? They really were *so*, those garbage cans were. So outdate. So ugly. So waste. And when those scavengers were taken into account, being *too*, well, then, any city accountant could do the math: *so* plus *too* equals *lose*, every time. The consensus knew this. Garbage cans gone, scavengers left piss-poor unlucky, a city problem solved, money banked—send in the next problem and tell it to wipe its feet on the way in.

Which didn't help Julian any.

"I don't think I'll be able to find any bottles tonight," he told Stanton.

"Of course a guy like you won't. Other people will find them. They always do."

"Will you let me back on the bus?"

"And let that dime go? Think about that. How can I do that? How can I let that little dime go?"

"I gave you all my money."

"I'll pay the dime, Jerry," called Pokey.

"Hold up, will you?" said Stanton. "This is how I kick my heels. You keep yours grounded for now." Stanton looked down at Julian. "You lost your last, lonely, baby dime. I feel for you. You get me? I feel for you. Him back there," Stanton jerked his thumb toward Pokey, "he'd love to help you out. That guy wants to give you a break. That'd be nice, wouldn't it? You'd appreciate that kind of a break. Do you know what? I'd love a break like that. I'd really appreciate that. But I'm not talking about some five days' break snacked off in between two bundles of weekends. I want a break from everything. You know I have constant pain in my legs? Can you appreciate that? Can you appreciate my pain?"

"I'm sorry," said Julian.

Stanton mulled the apology over. "That doesn't help. Do you want to hit me yet?"

Julian was not prone to violence. He had never muscled anybody. He never voiced the angers that overcame his thoughts occasionally, thoughts that bubbled up during conversations between Julian and people who held any power. Those people who sat behind bulletproof windows, desks, or behind clipboards. All those official types, of all the different branches, of all the sorts of multi-, and national, and governmental, and corporate, who themselves didn't want to speak with Julian, and who Julian didn't want to speak to either. But sadly, each had to talk to the other because without one the other wouldn't exist. No, when faced with the outward verbal or minor physical violence,[15] Julian's response was to crumple into himself, taking and apologizing for the position he found himself in.

15 Degrees and examples of violence to help readers in altercations:
- Minor physical violence: pushing; foot-stepping; car-bumper-kissing; name-calling.
- Major physical violence: face-kicking; knifing; guns-a-blazing; bombs-booming; planes-striking.

He always felt that he was the spark that set the minor physical abuse off in the first place.

"I'm sorry if I caused your legs to hurt," Julian told Stanton.

"What? What're you talking about? Don't you dare apologize to me. I'm sticking the shaft to you. You get that? You got to hate my guts right now."

"I don't like you very much. Does that help?"

"You don't like me? That's the best you can give me?" Stanton knocked Julian's change down the hatch. "I want to be left alone. You get me?"

"That what your wife tells you?" called the tired voice from the back of the bus.

"I'm single," said Stanton.

"Figures," replied the voice.

Stanton waved Julian onto the bus. As Julian climbed the steps, Stanton said, "Have you ever danced by yourself?"

"Like at a fancy ball?" asked Julian.

Stanton was disgusted. "Get out of my face." Julian waited to see if he was really free to go. "Move along, I said. Your voice is starting to grate on me."

Unsteadily gripping the tops of seats to stay balanced, Julian moved down the aisle as the *Go-Go* wobbled into motion. He passed the words WASTE OF SPACE, which were plastered repeatedly end to end around the bus. This was part of the WASTE OF SPACE campaign, though what the campaign actually was, what idea was being sold, which product was the solution, or what company was branding themselves with the slogan was all long forgotten. The signs had been a start, a teaser, a promise of better to come, but somewhere between the brainstorming and the first payments to blanket all the *Go-Go* buses in the advertising loss of inspiration and loss of capital took swarm.

Stanton should have taken the posters down months ago—enough riders had asked him to—but he just couldn't bring himself to follow through. He liked how the signs meshed with the seats. The seats were a discolouration of browns, reds, paisleys, and light greens. The colours a representation of the various eras of Metraville. They were meant to have a uniform look for each new groovy *Wheels-A-Go-Go* fleet that rolled out. Eventually, these fleets all meshed into one. Part of a recycle-and-refurbish plan that ignored comfort, style, and bodily evolution. The synthetic-drug and high-roller era was slapped down with the oversized and frugal and the revolutionary and communal eras. All the different eras converging at once, sending the riders into emotional tailspins every time they stepped aboard. They had no anchor in the present. By the time their bus stops came, they were left blinking furiously outdoors, completely lost in time. *Where am I?* they wondered. *Am I still a child? Have I retired? Hello?*

Julian was too busy trying to avoid the black sludge that covered the bus floor to pay much attention to the interior of the bus. The muck he was avoiding was an accumulation of what the passengers brought on in the grooves of their shoes and what they shook off their clothes. Cleaning this up was another job Stanton had let slide. He figured that whatever could evaporate, let it go, and what was left, the sludge, let that soak up in the clothes and spirits of the riders. All that water that they're bringing on, let it all wash into their day.

His Customers: Can't you clean up around here?

Stanton: Should I?

His Customers: Yeah, you should.

Stanton: How's that again?

Stanton couldn't stop himself. He'd whip up his microphone and ask riders, "You soaked yet?" He'd push his riders until he got cursed out. Push them until they threw their lunches at him. Push them until, if he was lucky, they'd get so upset that he'd end up with a split lip or a blackened eye.

After the riders had lost control, they'd yell at him, wanting to know what the fuck his problem was. What they didn't get was that *the fuck* was their problem, not Stanton's. The riders were the ones falling apart. They were the ones who couldn't hold themselves together, who let their chump jobs, their pasty relationships, their chronic halitosis absorb them and think that that gave them the right to inflict their failures on everyone else, especially Stanton. That's why they brought out their *fucks*—their pockets, purses, grocery bags, smelly paperbacks, even their pores, were oozing with all those sweary *fucks* they held tightly until he dragged them out.

Let the floor muck slop round and round. That muck was probably the best thing the riders ever produced. Which left Julian, eyes down, watching as the muck soaked up into the tips of his already deeply slushed running shoes. He passed a set of chairs with a sleeping bag and pillow tied to a leg with a piece of plastic cord. He pushed aside a crumpled pile of newspapers and sat down on the edge of the seat.

In black marker, someone had written SAGGING ASS HERE on the brown and yellow chair. Julian ran his hand across the words and then checked his fingers to make sure the words didn't come off on his hand. A worse scenario could have seen the words branded to his ass—backwards, no less. The unconscious admittance of what he feared—that his sagging ass, his drooping behind—would be signing itself all over the city. His hands weren't smudged, so he sat more fully, more comfortably, in the chair.

From the chair beside him, Julian heard someone make a click noise. He looked up into the one good oval black eye of a ventriloquist's dummy. The dummy's bad eye was hidden under several unevenly splayed pieces of duct tape. And when the dummy attempted to wink at Julian, the eyelid got halfway down before it sprang up again into its skull.

"Why didn't you come back to sit with us, pally?"

asked the dummy.

The us, the other who the dummy was referring to, was the ventriloquist—this was Pokey, who lowered his head toward Julian. "Hello," Pokey said softly.

"Oh, yeah, sorry. I forgot we was going to start with formalities. Hi, pal," said the dummy.

"Hi," said Julian, afraid to say anything else, afraid not to say anything else too, but not knowing what, or how, to say anything.

"You ever kill a man?" asked the dummy.

"Armbruster! You got to approach a guy slow when asking him a question like that," said Pokey.

"I'm a doing...da...doeing...ra...me...." Armbruster shook his head to try getting himself back on script. His last strings of hair, a residue of a long-gone head of hair, bounced as he shook.

"You'll have to forgive my friend; he's not doing too well," said Pokey.

Armbruster nodded toward Julian. "What you in for?"

"I'm just riding the bus."

"Murder, eh? Level with me—the guy you plugged, he had it coming, didn't he?"

"Which guy?" asked Julian.

"There were more than one? Whoa, pal. I got to say, on first sight you don't amount to much. But there's no telling, I guess. Get that, Pokey? He's in here for multiples."

"I'm not in for anything," said Julian.

"That's right. You tell 'em. You hear that, copper? We're all innocents on this here train."

"But I never hurt anybody."

"I think you're serious."

"Of course he's serious. We're on a bus, Arm. We're not going to jail," said Pokey.

"What's that you say?"

"*We're on a bus.*"

"I thought that's what you said! Niagara Falls! I told you not to get me started on that. Niagara Falls! The very words—"

"This isn't a bit now, Arm. Nobody mentioned the Falls. That gag isn't funny to anybody anymore."

"But that guy...the stranger...he's the one...."

"He never said anything."

"I didn't say it," agreed Julian.

"Didn't say what?" asked Armbruster.

"Don't let him trick you," said Pokey.

"What you said," said Julian.

"Didn't I say Niagara Falls?" asked Armbruster.

"Yes."

"That's where you stole my girl! And I'm coming to get you. Slowly I turn. Step by step." Armbruster flipped his leg over the back of his chair, his arms up in fight stance, heading toward Julian. "*Ni-a-ga-ra Falls! Niagara Falls!*"

"It doesn't count if you say it," said Pokey.

"Yes it does."

"No. Someone in the audience has to say the words to make the routine work."

"But I can still do it, Poke. I can still do the bit."

"Arm, that bit is dead."

Julian had been inching his way out of his chair while Pokey and Armbruster argued. He was hoping to get to the front of the bus, grab the railing, and cling there until he saw a stop he liked. He knew he wasn't quite thinking his plan through. The edges of an idea, a group of actions that would unfold after he got to the front of the bus scratched at his iced brain. He saw himself kicking the bus' front doors. Then he was jumping from the moving vehicle. There was a snowbank in there somewhere as well. The thoughts solidified, unable to warm up in his head.

Before he was even up, even dealing head on with a bus breakout, Pokey's warm hand, with steady, reassuring grip, stopped him from moving forward. Julian had forgotten what human contact felt like.

"Don't let Armbruster scare you. He's not well. We'd like you to stay. We could both use your company."

Julian forgot what he was doing. There was warmth from this man. There was need from him. Someone needed Julian. Someone saw him and didn't look away. For a fleeting second, Julian no longer felt like he was falling. "I'm not in a hurry," he said to Pokey.

"Sit down then. Give your dogs a breather," said Pokey. He let go of Julian's wrist. Julian grabbed Pokey's hand back and held it tightly. "Okay, friend, let's smooth that pace down."

"I need your hand. I want that good warm feeling."

Pokey could feel the desperation in Julian's grip. He knew that need, the excitement of contact. He tried wriggling free of it. He had to escape. He banged their hands against the side of the chair. Let go, Pokey thought. I don't want any more connections. Let me be.

"How about we hold hands when my hands aren't so full." Pokey lifted Armbruster up, displaying his Ex-hibit A.

"You promise?" asked Julian.

"You bet," Pokey said.

But Julian still couldn't let go of Pokey's hand.

"Okay now," said Pokey.

Armbruster opened his eye. "Some of us are trying to get our beauty sleep. Not that either of your ugly mugs know anything about that."

They didn't pay attention to him. Julian was too busy pulling Pokey's hand toward him. Pokey pulled back. Both men were breathing heavily, neither having exerted themselves in ages.

"And they're off," said Armbruster. "With the left hand, weighing in at one hundred and forty pounds and dropping, the failure of radio and television guest spots, the best joke he ever told was the one he lived:

Pokey Flatiron. And with the right hand, weight unknown. Background unknown. Name unknown. Self-esteem looks pretty low. The zero without the mirror. The guy without the style. The pal—and this is judging by his face, folks—without the gal."

Armbruster got up close to Julian's ear. The click from Armbruster's jaw hinges nearly drowned out his whisper. "Am I missing anything?"

"What?" Asked Julian.

"He's not even listening to me. Watch this. Knock, knock?" Armbruster waited. No one answered him. "Who's there? Nobody. Nobody. Nobody's listening. You hear that, Pokey? Nobody's tuned in. They're all deaf. What? What's that you say? Are you there? Armbruster to people, do you read me?"

"Let me go, please. Arm's panicking," said Pokey.

Armbruster had covered his face with his hands. "Pokey, why won't you talk to me? I am talking to you. Quiet for a sec, I can't hear myself think. Arm? Arm, you there? Arm here, Pokey. I know, I can see you. Well, if you can see me, why don't you answer me when I call you? I'm not listening. But can't you see my lips flapping uselessly? Sure I can. Well that's good, why not read 'em then?"

Pokey stuck his nails into Julian's hand, drawing blood. Julian let go. As he caught his breath, he watched Pokey cradle Armbruster in his arms.

Pokey whispered in Armbruster's ear, "Come here

often?"

"If I'd known you'd be here, I wouldn't have come at all," replied Armbruster.

"I was just making conversation," said Pokey.

"Conversation? Your voice is like a knife being jabbed in my ear."

"People have said my voice has that effect."

"Bet they say more than that. More than...right? More than...."

Armbruster passed out. Pokey wrapped him tightly in the blanket.

"At least I can get a word in edgewise." Pokey said.

"How do you stay so warm?" asked Julian, disappointed that they weren't still holding hands.

"We haven't gotten off this bus in weeks."

"But doesn't he," Julian whispered, gesturing toward Stanton, "doesn't he make you go outside?"

"We've come to an arrangement."

"A money arrangement?"

"Not everything ends in money. But seriously, germ, what's your vision like?"

Julian squinted at Pokey, hoping to see what Pokey really meant. "I can see."

"Can you see in the dark?"

"I guess."

"What can you see out of those windows right now?"

Julian couldn't see anything out the dirt-stiff windows. He didn't want to say this though. He was afraid if he put himself in another negative situation (the hand-holding incident obviously not having put him in the best light) that would be one letdown too many for Pokey. Then Pokey might not want to have anything to do with Julian anymore. "I see some buildings. There's snow."

"You can see better than I thought."

"What am I supposed to be looking for?"

"Forget about *looking for*. Everybody's always looking for something. I've got something for you to watch."

The bus began rocking back and forth. "Steady the bus, you worthless piece of shit," Pokey yelled to Stanton.

"You want to make something of it?" asked Stanton.

"You'll get something if I come up there."

"I love something. Something's the best thing I ever got. Can I have two somethings?"

Julian looked from Pokey toward Stanton. He tried tugging on Pokey's arm, a light, hey-stop-this-right-this-instant tug. Pokey jabbed Julian back in the ribs.

"Relax. This is just part of my service. Isn't that right?" he called up to Stanton.

"I still want something. I was promised something."

Pokey waved his fist in the air. "How about that as a down payment?"

"I do love down payment somethings."

Pokey laid Armbruster in a two-seater nearby. He pulled up three extension cords from the floor that were attached to two blocks of wood. One of the blocks was the length, the other the width, of the seats, and they acted as a barrier around Armbruster. Pokey tied the cords around the backs of the chair then patted the blocks to make sure they were sturdy. "Now, come here," he said to Julian. "I want you to see this."

He led Julian to the back of the bus. Jammed into the corner was a bulging knapsack, and wedged against the knapsack was a flattened plastic grocery bag. He took the bag out, turned it upside down, and shook all the contents out onto the back seats. There were cassette tapes, thick stacks of paper with butterfly clips fastened to them, a wig, fake moustaches, cue cards, bubble gum, newspaper clippings, and a plastic cup. Pokey proudly stretched his arms to encapsulate the mass.

"This is Arm and me. This is our career. Honestly, I think I did a great job of weeding out all the rotten jokes and bad routines we'd been holding onto. You know the ones you keep saying you'll get back to one day to make funny? I mean, at some point you realize, why hold onto the bit about the nun and the porcupine? It just doesn't work. And that's what I did. I junked them. All the bad jokes. The bad reviews. The low billings on marquee posters. What's left are all our winnings."

Pokey held up a cassette tape. The picture on the front was of Armbruster dressed as a doctor with a stethoscope around his neck and Pokey in a patient's gown. The title underneath them read SHUT UP & SPEAK.

"The college stations were crazy for this tape. We even got some airplay on a few big commercial stations. That was in '87, when we were experimenting with silences."

Pokey held up a newspaper clipping. In the picture, Pokey, with his back to Armbruster, was sharpening a knife while Armbruster approached him with an axe. "This picture, plus the tape, got us those commercials for Choco Fibres. You know those commercials, right? I'd say, 'I can't believe I'm eating fibre?' Arm went, 'I hate fibre.' Then I'd go, 'Yeah, but you know we both need it.' Then we both patted our bellies. That's when Arm killed with, 'And how.' Those two words, I'm not joking you, those two words kept us working for years."

Pokey absently picked at a hole in the armpit of his brown sweater. "Now, the only unfinished project we've kept is...." He searched through the pile and pulled up a navy Duo-Tang. "This. This is our screenplay *Sweet Nothings*. Picture it. We wander through the city streets, picking up dead-end jobs as we go. Here a dollar, there a dollar. Both of us searching for love, for happiness. The usual business.

"Anyway, the last shot is after we've been fired from

a plumbing gig. We've made a total cock-up of the thing: left taps spraying water, a bathtub through the floor, a boss soaking wet. And the last shot the audience would see is just us, sitting on a wall. It starts raining, so we put up our umbrellas. The umbrellas don't work, of course, but we hold them up anyway. And Arm turns to me and says, 'How you doing, pal?' To which I reply, 'I'm okay.' And Arm finishes with, 'Yeah, me too.'"

Pokey put the screenplay back on top of the pile. "I've totally lost my train of thought," he said. "What did I want to say?"

Don't say it. Don't say the thought that's in your head, Pokey thought. What good is thinking when it'll take a person where he was going? And anyway, thoughts were meant to be kept to themselves. Talk up a thought and the thought was no longer thought. Pokey would have to say sentences, and those sentences would lead to ideas, and then sentences and ideas would lead to verbal agreements, verbal agreements to actions, and actions to repercussions. Couldn't he and this dripper that was standing before him, couldn't they have a silent agreement, a nod-to-nod contract, the unsaid remaining unsaid but agreed upon? Pokey nodded to Julian. Julian nodded back. There we go, thought Pokey, deal done. No fifteen percent taken off. No bum contracts this time out.

"I don't know," said Julian.

"Sorry? What? What don't you know? Are you talking about our nods? We've agreed now."

"I meant I don't know what you were trying to say. That's the last thing you said before going silent."

"Don't worry what I was trying to say. Let's let my thoughts remain silent but agreed upon. You follow me?"

"No."

"Okay. Fine. Do you know how to be a witness?"

"A witness of what?"

How to explain the role of the witness? Pokey took a deep breath. "You know...uh...you just stand and watch something. No, that isn't quite it. Okay, say you see something go down. Like someone, I don't know, hits a guy with a spoon. Then the cops would ask you, 'Who hit who?' And that's being a witness. This is hard enough for me. I'm asking for help. I can't do it alone. You understand? I mean what's the problem? Is it money? Do you want me to pay you? I got some money. Would, say, twelve dollars be enough? Some bucks in pennies. Dollars in nickels. All filled up in a pickle jar."

"What are you paying me for?"

"For the witness job. I need help with Arm. I mean, look at him. He needs to sleep."

"Would you quit talking in euphemisms? Just spit out the truth for once. Just say it," said Armbruster.

"I'm doing my best here," said Pokey.

"That's probably why you're not getting anywhere."

"Say yes," Pokey told Julian.

Julian didn't think he had a choice. "Yes. To what exactly?"

"No. You said yes. Good. Perfect. We kill Arm in an hour."

"Kill?" said Julian.

"But not right now. That's the key point. In an hour."

"Please report to the front of the bus," said Stanton over the bus speakers. "I want you to get a load of something."

"We're busy," said Pokey. "There are serious negotiations going on back here."

"I got a show about to start."

"The show's back here."

"Well, there's another show that I want to show."

"Why would we want to see your show?"

"Because I'm a show. I'm a warm-up act."

Someone knocked on the front doors of the bus. Stanton giggled.

Julian's brain was still an icebox. He pretended he hadn't heard Pokey right. They shuffled to the front of the bus. Stanton opened the doors. Standing single file in a snowbank, shivering, were two round men. The two men began clapping when the doors opened.

Julian knew these men. Everyone that still roamed the city by foot and vehicle (without the aid of heavy window tinting) knew this type of person. *Scavengers.*

The name stuck in people's throats. They wanted to call the scavengers thieves, burglars, criminals. But *oh no*, that was *too* strong. Those associations reflected poorly on the tourist trade. You couldn't call the scavengers thieves! Not in a great spit-shine clean city like Metraville, said the city beauticians.

Even the scavengers themselves felt the name focused too heavily on the negative connotations of their trade.[16]

Lately, even the name "scavengers" wasn't good enough. Wrong connotations, apparently. The scavengers were heavily arguing among themselves that they should be seen as the new explorers, hunting and discovering among the treasures of the nearly departed city. To their minds, they were the front line of urban planners. No, damn it, that wasn't sophisticated enough. They were *the* metropolitan cartographers. Or, what the scavengers were really hoping would catch on with the gen pop, their nomenclature of choice was *cartopolitans*.

---

16 A moment of public reaction:

"*You hear that, Mavis? The news is saying them scavengers are a trade profession now.*"

"*You don't say, Nellie?*"

"*I do. They all just up and had themselves a press conference stating as such.*"

"*Not just a press conference by the looks of things.*"

"*That's right. They've got letter-writing campaigns, television advertisements.*"

"*And a rally!*"

"*It's got so that everyone has got to feel sticks-and-stones guilty about the name-calling.*"

Worse still, what really irked Metravillians was how annoyingly likeable the scavenger folks were. They, as a group, were one of the most well-mannered in the city. Just as sure as they'd steal the lid off a person's milk bottle, the scavengers would help another across the road in inclement weather (nicking the person's shoelaces, of course, but really, one good service deserves a small tripped tip).

"Very nice to see you again, Monsieur Stanton," said one of the scavengers.

Before the scavenger could get his foot up on the first step, Stanton said, "Where do you think you're going, Tony?"

"Now, now, Monsieur Stanton. You know full well that my name is Antony."

"Sorry about that, Tony."

"What's about?" said the second scavenger as he pulled a plastic bag tighter over his head. "We're very much chilled, good sir."

"Tobias, I've sad news to report. I suspect we won't be travelling by motor this night," said Antony.

"I concur in totality, Antony. Seems we are at your disadvantage as always, sir," said Tobias to Stanton.

"My disadvantage must really be grating on you guys," said Stanton.

Ignoring him, Tobias said, "I feel we are out of luck, Antony."

"I believe so, Tobias. I do believe so."

"Antony, have you mentioned that we have funds?"

"Funds? That's new news," said Stanton. "I wish you'd said so from the start. We could have avoided all these needless arguments we've been having. Hop on, friends."

The bus had started moving forward slowly. To keep up with it, Antony and Tobias had to run, with Tobias holding the back of Antony's trench coat so he wouldn't step on it.

"This is beneath Tobias and I, sir. Simply beneath us."

"You are a sight for failed efforts," called Tobias.

"You're a pair of huffing and a-puffing stains," replied Stanton.

"And you are wilting away worse every night," said Antony.

"*Ha.* I'll be the first one spitting on your ashes."

"Ashes? Antony and I are not pedestrian chaps. We've invested in a pair of double plots."

"Though, Tobias, I believe we really must think on a grander scale."

"Are you still mulling the sepulchre?" asked Tobias.

"I'm always mulling the sepulchre over."

Tobias and Antony stopped running. The bus passed them and kept going. They placed the plastic bags they'd wrapped around their wrists between their feet and took out several of the bigger chunks of rock they'd found while exploring. Tobias' aim had always been the better of the two, and with ease, he smacked one, two, four rocks against the bus, adding three more cracks to the already spreading web on the back window.

Antony, for his part, was able to lob an empty bottle on top of the bus, where it exploded.

"I believe that's the best shot you've ever had," said Tobias.

"Agreed. I've been setting my sights on that mark for weeks."

"The top? You've never said anything about this before."

"I wanted to surprise you."

They picked up their bags and began walking, side by side, in the opposite direction of the departing bus.

"What made you fixate on the roof?" asked Tobias.

"Deductive logic."

"I'm intrigued."

"I knew you would be. I've watched you chip away at those windows for some time and a thought occurred to me. If I'm not as accurate as you, then I need to expand my sights. The roof felt like the next best—"

"And broader—"

"Exactly. But even more than that—"

"Oh what immense thinking. I can barely breathe with—"

"We can weaken the infrastructure of the bus in two places."

"How long have you kept this wonderfulness from me?"

"A mere six weeks."

"Your excitement must have been excruciating."

"You can't imagine."

"We must find more bottles. Though, I say, with all this talk of infrastructure, I've come back to a thought. Imagine one major onslaught, one of us on either side of the street, undiscovered until we begin pounding that tired beast. Monsieur Stanton would crumple at last."

"Then our games would end. We'd lose the sport."

"Yes. You're right, Antony. That is the point I always manage to misplace."

"You do always like to rush through."

"I know. I know."

"And you really shouldn't. Not when your heart beats at such speeds."

"My heart does rip to its own, rather peculiar, rhythms."

From the front step of his stopped bus, Stanton watched the two men as they walked into the swirling snow, straining to hear them long after they had disappeared.

An Intermission with Young Master Pokey:
An Officer and a Lady[17]

A knees-shaking teenaged Pokey wobbles out onto the stage. "Sorry to disturb everyone. I promise we'll return to the show in just a second. The stage manager has asked me to come out to see—is everyone comfortable?"

At this point, given a moment's reflection, some audience members give their predictable catcalls. "Get off the stage." "I don't want to hear no child." "You're dirty behind the ears." Pokey always bows rather than respond. Be gracious, his mother always says. Don't lose your audience in speared retorts and tongue-bashings.

Pokey asks again, "Is there anyone out there, anyone at all, who doesn't like where they're sitting?"

The members of the audience look at each other suspiciously. Has someone complained? Was the per-

---

17 An Officer and a Lady was Pokey's first, original, three-voice act. He'd had hours to himself while his parents practiced and performed their magic act. He'd sit alone in their dressing room, a clothespin snapped to the middle of his lips, practicing. The idea for the Officer and the Lady was lifted from the duelling couple, his Uncle Charlie and Auntie Beckie (road relations, not blood), who themselves had a type of Officer-and-the-Lady act. Their couple was always coming apart, chasing one another on stage, getting each other behind bars.

Pokey had refined, expanded, perfected his Officer and Lady act until Armbruster was given to him by a desperate and job-loss-fearing Uncle Charlie.

son beside me not happy to sit with me? they wonder.

"Well, I'm not hearing anyone, so I guess—"

A man's muffled voice *mmm-hmmed* from somewhere in the middle of the audience.

"Oh, there is someone," said Pokey.

The man kept up his *mmm-hmming*, and another muffled voice, this time a woman's, began *hmm-hmming*. The audience began their own *buzz-buzzing*.

"If I could ask everyone to remain calm. Sir," Pokey pointed to a man, always a man, "if you would kindly lift your bum off your seat." The men never questioned the proceedings. They stood up quickly and obediently, afraid they accidentally sat on someone. And as they stood up, out from under their behinds, came a voice:

"Talk about bad air," the Officer told the audience. "I should bring him up on charges of indecent air exposure."

Pokey pointed at a woman, always a woman, always an ample-breasted woman at the other side of the auditorium. "Madame, if you wouldn't mind shaking out your top."

The woman protested, "I certainly will not."

The muffled woman's voice *hmm-hmmed* even louder. Pokey began to sound panicked. "Please, Madame, I'm worried you might be suffocating her."

This always got the woman moving. Like a bee in the bonnet with a sting close to skin, the woman began shaking her collar, trying to fan the voice to safety. To add to the excitement, the Officer, from the other end of the auditorium, said, "What's this about an attempted suffocation?"

Pokey waited, waited, waited for the woman to stand up. He waited for the woman to realize she was making a spectacle of herself, that she might be holding up the performance, that she might in fact, Lord knows how, be killing someone. And when she stood up, out came another voice:

"Why, I never," said the Lady.

"You never what?" called the Officer.

"I never imagined I'd get out of those mountains," she said.

"If the voices of the Officer and the Lady would please come to the front," said Pokey.

As the voices came up onto the stage, they continued their conversation. "You mean the Lady and the Officer," said the Lady.

"She's right, son," said the Officer. "Ladies first."

"And how do you know I'm a lady?" said the Lady.

"Well, you just identified yourself as such."

"Come now, Officer, I'm sure you can do better than that."

"You shouldn't tell a policeman how to do his job."

"Oh, and what was I suggesting?"

The voices were almost beside each other. "Well, I know what I'd be suggesting."

"And what's that."

"This is that." The Officer kissed the Lady. The smooch could be heard throughout the auditorium.

"Well, I never," said the Lady.

"Never what?" asked the Officer.

"Never knew how good a lover you could be."

Their heavy petting began in earnest—the noises bounding around the stage. "Maybe you two should get a room," said Pokey.

"Are you crazy?" said the Officer.

"What's wrong with that?" asked Pokey.

"Have you seen the price of rooms?" responded the Lady.

"I'm afraid they have a point, ladies and gentlemen. For the rest of the performances, please pay no heed to the hanky panky happening to the—"

"Left of the stage," said the Officer.

"Oh, I'm sure we'll make it to the right as well," said the Lady.

"Let's hope so," said the Officer.

*

From his open bus doors, Stanton watched as Pokey, Armbruster wrapped in a blanket, and Julian descended the hill into Base Park. He'd tried going with them, but one tip of the toe on the unsteady ground had reassured him there was nothing going for a man like himself out there. Not anymore, that was for sure.

Better to stay on his bus, his legs up on the steering wheel, with maybe a passerby or a long-lost traffic cop to keep him occupied.

Meanwhile, Pokey, Armbruster, and Julian walked obliviously through Base Park's history.[18] They climbed the hill at the other end of Base and descended into Glant Park. Once known for its manicured flowerbeds; its stone paths; and its centrepiece, the proud, deuce-loving, "I say, son, nice backhand," "You're too kind

---

18 Base Park was the stopgap, the intermission that people used to pass through on their way to Glant Park or Oblong Park. All that constituted Base Park was a mess of grass and mud. There were no picnics held, no wedding photographs taken, no animals that dared inhabit that disused air of the city. Generations of city planners had wiped their bottoms in defo-dynamite contruction plans for Base that they were sure could rock the metropolis to its core. That Base, though, that confound-it Base, with its nowhere space, undermined all their payola dreams.

Base's origins were set down in bones. Underneath the park were not just ancient burials, snuffed-out adversaries, and time capsules jam-packed with blackmailed booty, but there were also pipes, generators, console rooms, and printer-and-spool running computers that kept the meters running and the street lights clicking. There was heart-of-the-city-business happening under the park that spread from Base out to the edges of Oblong and Glant, making construction completely impossible.

That impossibility created a sense of foreboding around the parks and went a long way to explaining why people didn't bother with them anymore. Signs that had been stuck up at the entrances and exits, the WELCOME TO and SEE YOU AGAIN signs, had become the victims of traffic accidents and unimaginative teenage scrawlings. People talked dismissively of the parks. The parks were nothing special. They were one after the other after the other across some roads. The general consensus was that the public didn't want to get mixed up in any shifty park lifestyles.

me, lad" tennis and lawn bowling club, now Glant was trapped among the cobwebs.

Pokey led them past the club. As they went deeper into the park, they left behind the sparse but passing traffic, the motion detectors and insomniacs awake in their houses and condos, and the burning office lights in the skyscrapers that could afford to keep their energy on.

Julian thought he was used to silence, but he couldn't adjust himself to the natural terrain. Over the

---

This hostility had built up plot of grass by unconscious plot of grass over the twelve reigning years of Mayor Hal "Everybody's a Pal Of" Grant's life in office. Hal had railed against park life whenever he had the opportunity. For him, parks weren't hikes, picnics, outdoor games, or heavy petting; they were the last refuge of closet pornographers, and public poopers, and all those dopers with their illicit drugs he was always being tempted with.

What was never discussed, what everybody had forgotten, was that Hal had successfully inseminated in one of those "*mud patches of the masses*" (Hal's inflection). His success had produced two illegitimate twin sons who were frightfully identical to their father. Hal tried to hide them with lump sums of cash to their mother, but the resemblance was too eerily close, very much clone Cs of Pal Hal. The fact that their mother named them Cal and Mal didn't help Hal any.

As Hal tried to explain, those boys were a minor point in a very private, very painful, episode in his life that had nothing to do with the public, nothing to do with his decision making in regards to the city, and definitely nothing to do with any damn parks. Hal made a passionate speech along these lines when the boys' existence was unearthed. He even attempted to apologize to "those bastards...excuse me, my boys..." while standing arm in arm with his legitimate family on the grounds of a brand new family-friendly mixed space condominium complex to be built on the remains of what was once known as Factory Park (the same park that the sons were conceived in).

last month, he'd walked through sections of Metraville where movement was rare. Blocks of car garages, factories, eateries, laundromats, and second-storey apartments had lost the battle of attrition, as their usefulness had been first restructured, then abandoned.

The emptiness on those streets was nothing like the park's. Errant light bulbs burned in those factory halls, exit signs were lit red over diner back doors, and four-way street lights still winked on and off. There were echoes of the street's former life. The parks didn't even offer those fleeting reassurances for Julian.

As he watched Pokey effortlessly step over exposed tree roots and jump off rocks, Julian felt his isolation magnify. Pokey had turned the art of night walking into a form of dance, shedding the locked knee stumbling of Julian, who practically tripped over every step. "Mr. Pokey," he called. "How far are we headed?"

"Shh," whispered Pokey. "Don't disturb the park. We'll talk when we reach—"

"Hello?" a female voice with a British accent called from some distance away.

"Who's that?" asked Julian.

Pokey slapped his hand over Julian's mouth. He pushed his shush finger over his open palm to reinforce his point.

"Excuse me, but some of us are trying to sleep," said the Lady, now much closer to them.

A male voice, also British, came from another direction in the woods. "What's all this then?"

"This then," this was the Officer and the Lady. At Armbruster's request, Pokey and his father had taken the Lady and the Officer out to Glant and buried them in the woods.

Buried until—

"Oh, Officer. I've been disturbed," said the Lady.

"A disturbance. What sort? Is it a murderous disturbance?"

"I didn't hear a killing."

"So not a murder? Best be moving on then."

"Well...if you must."

"How's that, ma'am?"

"Well it is awfully cold out here."

"'Tis cold. 'Tis at that."

"You'd be more than welcome to stop in for a spell."

"I'd be very much obliged. I'm by myself so much since the wife legged it."

"You're not spoken for then?"

"Can't say that I am. And what might your situation be?"

"My husband has passed."

"Ah. Excellent."

The tree branches clapped against one anther.

"Care for some tea?" asked the Lady.

"I'd love a cup."

"May I offer you some little cakes?"

"How can I refuse?"

"I think these will be to your liking."

"These aren't cakes."

"And that's not your leg."

Pokey pushed Julian along and away from the gabbing Officer and Lady, whose voices began to drift off. He didn't want the voices to disturb Armbruster, to reawaken jealousies or start the "stop speaking for them" tangents that he and Arm used to circle around. Just as the voices were about to be out of earshot completely, Armbruster said, "What're you doing? I was almost finished."

"What do you mean almost finished?" asked Pokey.

"I don't mean dead. I'm talking about jerking off."

"Jesus, Arm, not on my hand. And you can stop now anyway. You won't be hearing them again."

"Hear who?"

"The Lady and the Officer."

"Who's that?"

"The Officer and—"

"Do you mean the pervs getting off in the bush we just heard?"

"Yes."

"Then why didn't you just say so?"

Pokey realized they weren't going to have their old argument. He was disappointed. Arm's trigger putdowns, his fast recall, all that was muck now. And that muck had nearly evaporated. But as if on cue, as if his powers of timing were fighting to get to the stage for one more show, Arm said, "Quit wasting my time here. I'm tired of feeling sick—let's get this over with."

Pokey liked the sound of that. Imagine, all over with. Fini. The curtain closes with a final THE END. Come on, Pokey, Pokey told himself. You're almost free of this. Push a little more. Then the burden is— He didn't mean that. Not like that. Pokey didn't want to get rid of. Not dispose of. When he only thought of a word like *burden*, he only thought that because of all the pressure he was under. He was suffocating under it. He only thought that because.... That's right. Because. Because of just cause. The cause of exhaustion. The cause of cold. The cause of the never-ending cough and sputter. Arm and Burden. That would have made a great sketch.

Pokey stopped walking. "We go up here," he said, pointing up a hill.

He slung Armbruster over his shoulder, and started climbing. He pulled them up the hill easily, using the bushes that stuck out of the earth as handles. The snow on the hill was heavy, but underneath this, the ground was covered in leaves all layered and meshed like a thousand banana peels. As Julian climbed, his feet slip-slided from under him. He fell. Branches slapped him in the face. Warped trees hip-checked him with their trunks.

Midway up the hill, Pokey waited. Julian finally

rolled onto on his back on a path that was big enough for them to walk along it in single file.

Julian was tired of walking around. How long had he been doing this wandering business? Well, when was his last job? Yeah, when was that? He'd been between jobs for— *Between* really wasn't the right word. He had lost his occupation some time ago, but there weren't two positions he was wedged against. No one job lost and another a leap away. Nothing fixed in the distance. So thinking he was between jobs really gave him the wrong impression of where he was.

"Do you guys still work?" Julian asked.

"You making fun of us?" asked Armbruster.

"I didn't think so." He wasn't asking to make fun. He was trying to deflect, to put off thought about all this between business of his.

"We haven't worked in ages," said Pokey.

"Five hundred and twenty one ages," said Armbruster.

"But who's counting?"

"Not me, that's for sure." To prove this, Armbruster held up his left hand to show that he only had a thumb left. "If only we'd called ourselves 'Armbruster and Pokey.'"

"Don't start," said Pokey.

"I'm starting with you because I mention the alphabet?"

"I've told you a thousand times: you always start

with the shorter name on the marquee."

"No, you start with the star. Then the little guy."

"I wrote all the material."

"You were my secretary. You copied everything I said."

"Three quarters of our routines were written while you were asleep."

"And our routines were part of the problem."

"Our routines? No way. Your face is what did us in. Your disfigured poorly reconstructed face."

"That's down to you, man. You used glue, tape, gum, and staples. I begged you to get me fixed up with a carpenter. You should have taken action when you saw the ant crawl in my ear. You shouldn't have let all those kids molest me. You shouldn't have let that chick put my arm in her...."

They didn't even know Julian was there anymore. They were too busy working through their previous show. The show they showed without meaning to show it to their audiences. If there'd been 521 gaps since their last performance, that was because for the previous 50, when audiences laughed, they weren't enjoying tight cues or highly rehearsed bits. They were laughing at Poke and Arm—sorry, at Arm and Poke. They were the act who had suffered too long together. Their insulting banter had stopped long ago being part of the gag.

That ugly face, those poor routines, the girls who'd

turned away, hoping to speak with the stand-up comic instead of them, oh, those failures kept being thrown on top of Armbruster and Pokey until they suffocated under them. Until the last head shake, the lone hand-dismissal, the final strange body had emptied the audience of audience. After that, there was just the two of them. Now Baxter, the late discovery, was meant to be the final piece of their new act.

The three travellers stepped through a pair of bushes into a small clearing that was surrounded by trees. One barkless tree stood in the circle's midst. This space and this tree were where Armbruster and Pokey had pitched their last tent. They'd practiced, refined, rewrote, all gearing up for the perfect execution. All their glorious words had bounced around among the silence of the forest, all their steps leading to their final performance.

Suey Sides
(In which Armbruster and Pokey try to crack open that puzzling topic of youth in Asia)

Poke: What'd you think?

Arm: That tree is ugly.

Poke: (*to Julian*) What about you?

Julian: What am I supposed to say?

Arm: You guys are going to shoot me.

Poke: I forgot the gun. (*To Julian*) Are you packing heat?

Julian: No.

Arm: I'm feeling lucky already.

Poke: We've got other solutions.

Arm: A gun would have been faster.

Poke: But I haven't told you my other options.

Arm: I already won't like them.

Poke: Are you trying to talk me out of this?

Arm: Is it working?

Poke: No. I'm starting to like the idea of getting rid of you.

Arm: But why me? I don't owe you money.

Poke: True.

Arm: I didn't kill one of your family.

Poke: True again.

Arm: I didn't sleep with your wife.

Poke: ...

Arm: She wasn't your wife.

Poke: ...

Arm: And you were there.

Poke: I'll give you that.

Arm: Why snuff me? Why now?

Poke: Why not?

Arm: You raise an interesting argument. (*To Julian*) Do you agree with him?

Poke: (*To Julian*) Say yes. That's what I'm paying you for.

Arm: He's being bribed?

Poke: You got a problem with that?

Arm: No. I just wish I knew his rates so I could outbid you.

Julian: What am I supposed to do?

Poke: Strangle that man. (*Pokey and Armbruster point at one another*)

Arm: This is premeditated. This is dark circles. This is evildoing.

Poke: We're trying to put you out of your misery.

Arm: You can get rid of my misery?

Poke: (*Annoyed*) That's what we've been talking about.

Arm: Then I'm all yours. (*To Julian*) Now, throw this guy in the wood chipper and we'll get out of here.

Julian smacks his hand against his face.

Julian: Will one of you please tell me who I'm supposed to kill?

Poke & Arm: Take him.

Arm & Poke: No, take him.

Poke: You.

Arm: Me?

Poke: See? He agrees.

Arm: You're picking on me because I'm lame.

Poke: Why else would I get rid of you?

Arm: Because you've always resented my fame.

Poke: I did all the legwork.

Arm: You know I would have helped if my legs weren't floppy.

Pokey hands Armbruster to Julian.

Poke: Hold him while I make a noose.

Arm: You're going to hang me?

Poke: I'm out of options. We don't have a gun. No sword. The wood chipper was too heavy. I don't know how to spark a fire. Can't deep-fry you. The beetles and mites refuse to play their part. Age hasn't beaten you. What am I left with but old-fashioned rope-tied death?

Pokey bends down and begins unlacing his shoelace.

Arm: (*To Julian*) How could you do this to me?

Julian: I don't want to hurt anybody.

Arm: Does that anybody include me?

Julian: I thought you were sick.

Arm: Why does that mean I've got to go for the big sleep?

Julian: You said you wanted to go.

Arm: Of course I do. But I want to go out in style. A twenty-one gun salute. Maidens by my bed. A priest. A rabbi. A call from the warden. Not like this. Not in some back alley at the hands of a couple of idiots.

Poke: No one gets to choose how they go.

Arm: You make a point.

Poke: Finally, we agree.

Arm: I said you make one. I just don't like its tip.

Poke: (*To Julian*) Hold him up.

Julian lifts Armbruster up to the branch. Pokey ties one end of the lace around Armbruster's neck. He then ties the other around the branch.

Poke: Put him on my shoulders.

Julian rests Armbruster on Pokey's shoulders. Pokey reaches his arm around and presses his hand against Armbruster's back to steady him.

Arm: Folks, syrup and candy sparkles make the loveliest couple.

Poke: (*To Armbruster*) What're you saying?

Arm: Can't you hear me?

Poke: My hearing's going.

Arm: Where's it going?

Poke: On a date with that man's wife. (*He points at Julian*)

Julian: I'm not married.

Arm: (*To Pokey*) Your hearing might be going, but my eye is still working. Take my advice, anyone who finds this guy attractive must be even worse off than he is.

Poke: Not worse than you. This is the end of your line.

Arm: I did want kids, you know. I just couldn't keep up. Everything went by too quickly.

Poke: Are you done stalling?

Arm: Done? That's how I've managed to keep on living.

Poke: Here we go.

Arm: Wait. Hold up. Don't I get any last remarks?

Poke: You've said enough.

Pokey steps forward. Armbruster falls behind him, his body swinging from the lace attached to the tree.

*

If Pokey had a curtain to pull shut, he would have done so. As they'd rehearsed it, their *Suey Side* pact was now delivered. All that was left were several twitchy movements, a few sputtered coughs, maybe a final "Hail Jesus" from Arm to leave the crowd with something to take home to mum. But Arm didn't say anything. His final joke, unplanned like the best of them, was that his eye and left arm popped out at the impact of being let go. The body parts dropped into the snow. One last finger salute, Pokey thought as he shook his head over the mess.

"You're our audience. You got to clap."

Julian began to clap slowly. "Is this how you like?"

"Put some life into it, man."

Julian clapped harder. The sound echoed in the forest.

"Harder, man. Come on. One potato, two potato, hit potato more. I'm the show, I love the show, I wish the show galore." Pokey began hopping from one foot to the other. He clapped as well. "Join me. Hop with me."

Julian began hopping.

"Repeat after me," said Pokey.

Julian waited. Pokey gestured to him that this was the point at which he was to start.

"Repeat...after...me?" said Julian.

"Exorcist, sexorcist, nipples, and sticks."

"Exorcist, sexorcist, nipples, sticks."

"You forgot the *and*."

"You forgot the *and*."

"No. You forgot the *and*."

"No. You forgot the *and*."

"Stop repeating me." Pokey stopped hopping to emphasize his meaning. "All I was trying to say was that you weren't doing the bit properly."

"I've never done a bit properly."

"I can tell."

"Do you want me to try again?"

"What's the point? You need decades of training. We need an exercise bike. There would be all-night cram sessions. Puddles of coffee. Whiskey habits. Who has the energy for that dedication? At my age, I'm usually asleep by ten. Up by nine. Where does that leave time for comedy and pornography?"

"You make blue movies?"

"I'm talking about girl-watching. Theatre of the mind stuff. Arm and I wanted a skin flick. We even wrote a nudie movie. But we couldn't get any money for a trenchcoat production about a dummy. We felt it was better to stick to private pornography. But back to facts. Please, this is the only gig you'll ever do. You were a star; now move along. The dancing ladies are up next."

Armbruster farted.

"What was that?" asked Julian.

"The final evacuation," said Pokey. He bowed his head. He noticed Julian hadn't bowed his head. "Come on. A moment of silence for our fallen brother."

Far off, drifting on the wind, reverberating off the shaking bare branches, transmitted on the radiations of the rising sun, came the sound of traffic. Lone birds began to tweet, to call, to search for others. Straining hard, Julian swore he heard a baby crying. Maybe this was the call of a newborn, using its pipes for the very first time.

"Is this heaven?" asked Armbruster.

"No, Armbruster, you're still alive," said Pokey.

"Thank God. I'd hate to think the afterlife sounds this terrible."

"Is he alive?" asked Julian.

"Yes, I'm alive," said Armbruster.

"Do we have to murder him again?"

"Murder him?" asked Pokey. "You think we're common psychos? We're not rusty blades and grubby hands."

"Jokes and art," said Armbruster.

"Definitely jokes," replied Pokey.

"And Art?" asked Armbruster.

"Art not so much."

"Not at all."

"Should we have added him?"

"Art's so difficult to work with."

"He's not vital at all."

"That reminds me. I forgot to take my vitals before you hung me."

"You'll have to have them when we get back to the bus."

"I can't let my health slide."

"I agree. One can never be too careful."

"Never indeed."

"I've never told you this, but I lost the deed years ago."

"How?"

"Poker game."

"You bet the farmer too?"

"And his daughter."

"Well, she wasn't much to look at."

"Who was looking?"

"Not me, now that I'm blind," said Armbruster.

Pokey had been rummaging in the snow as he riffed

with Armbruster. He found the arm, and after much scanning, found the eyeball staring up at him silently asking, "What took you so long?" He picked it up between his index and baby finger and carried it and the arm to Julian.

"Get these out of his sight," whispered Pokey. "We need space to rehearse. These will only get in the way. Shoo. Fly. We'll never get anything done with an audience. Think of it. We've got ourselves a whole new blind act to practice. Who knows where this will take us? But with prying ears like yours, we'll never get a word in edgewise."

"What'll you do?"

"What we usually do. We'll practice until noon. Then us and Stanton will grab some dinner before crashing in some parking lot to sleep."

"Money for some pour," called Armbruster.

"What're you drinking?" asked Pokey.

"Whatever's dumped in my mouth."

"That's your punchline?" said Pokey.

"No good?"

"Not even a featherweight would have thrown that."

"I blame the manager."

"Oh do you?!" Pokey stormed over to Armbruster.

As Julian left them, Pokey was throwing his arms up, while Armbruster yelled back. About halfway along the little path, he fell down the hill. At the bottom, he found himself on a new path. This one was much wider. He followed this in some direction (the norths, those wests, were never markers Julian was sure of). After much walking, the path curved upward and out onto the street. This was a new street, nowhere near where they had entered the park from originally.

He needed to cover Armbruster's parts properly if they were going to be walking around together. Someone might mistake them for human body parts. By the time he'd be able to explain himself, the police and medics would have gotten involved, statements would have been given, and many children would have been frightened. Better to just hide the arm and eye under his coat. As he was about to cover up Armbruster's pieces, Julian noticed that they were all cracked up. The eye had broken in two. The arm was nearly dust. Had this happened when Julian fell down the hill? Maybe when the arm fell out of the tree? Whatever the reason, fatal breaks had been made.

As he made his way through the city, Julian left the pieces of Armbruster in places he thought Armbruster and Pokey would have appreciated. He laid one finger on someone's chair in a diner. Part of the eye he slipped into a woman's coat pocket while she waited for the light to turn. The other part of the eye he buried in a potted tree on a main street. The rest he scattered behind him in the fresh snow as he tried to find his way home.

19:33 ● 19:38

Dog owner
routinely flings
canine shit at
diner window,
    yelling about
their poisons.

February 29

11:16 ● 13:05
Unicycle-bike
crash. They told
the copper all
'just an accident.
Really, each staked
a corner, Rode at
each other again &
again, 'in games
of chicken. I
figure the unicyclist
had the edge.

January 12

Sign in store
window reads
FIRE, WILL OPEN
AGAIN IN/WHEN
SMOKE HAS CLEARED.
Through the window,
just an empty store.
This has been going
on for over a year.

THE METRAVILLE HALL OF FAME AWARDS

Big Doll House Propaganda Department: Matthew Pollack

Champion of First Races: Debra Di Blasi

Department of Family Initiatives: Harry Popowich; Pia Corston; Ann Popowich; Tim Popowich; Dan Popowich

Entertainment Consultant: Nicole Stavroff

League of Editors, Fire Breathers, Honesty Meters: Jon Paul Fiorentino

Memory Exporter: Dave Fiore

Peaceful Crowd Control: Mary Esteve

Political Chairman: Mike O'Connor

Sanitation Department: Dan Varrette

Committee of the Unknown Origins: Gillian Rodgerson

Road and Safety Removal: Gillian Urbankiewicz

Savvy Sage: Michael Burn

Our Good Samaritans: Enriqué Gaudité; Kathy Howat; Mike Knox; Ian Krykorka; Mark Laurie; Lynn McClory; Eva Moran; Ali Muhumed; Alexandra Pasian; Graeme Slaght; Grandma Rose; Rebecca Rosenblum; Jenny Sampirisi; Siri Segaram; Mary Lou Stavroff; Aaron Tucker; Jason Wells

Union Honesty Review: Jim Corston

The Golden Banana Peel Slip goes to the always astonishingly slapstick Angela Szczepaniak, who argues a good cause, supports the reckless endeavour, agrees with aged and regular aged cats, and is Metraville's First Writer Laureate. The honour is all Metraville's!

Let Metraville take a moment to applaud all our winners. Also, to all our Metravillians, we promise the roads will be fixed.

Some of the Metraville public you have just read about appeared in other periodicals. Metraville would like to thank *In Posse Review* and *And/Or*.

The Banana Peels Maestro was kind enough to give me permission to record two of his performances for my Metraville archives.

The images of Ham the Astrochimp and Joseph Kittinger are graciously freefloating in the public interether. Mr. Kittinger was not headed for Metraville. And Ham the Astrochimp never did any official publicity in Metraville.

Supplemental List of Aerial Concerns

Anvils
Pianos
Falling men
Jumping women
Potted plants
Bricks
Arrows
Cats
Dogs
Acorns
Trees
Buildings
Satellites
Asteroids
Stars
Planets

Banana peels everywhere. They make midnight calls to your mother. Your girlfriend's tone is tinged with them. Little children count them before they fall asleep. The oldest living peel is 142. A peel drove a couple, by cab, to the airport yesterday. They are the new dirty bomb. Small-minded bureaucrats have been making cuts to peels for years. Throughout history, peels have appeared in the backgrounds of paintings. Early television sets were fitted with them for antennae. Way back in the nineteenth century, farmers in Saskatchewan tried to grow a field variety for the masses. Legend has it that some sections of the New York sewers are awash with banana peels.

The highest-grade wigs are made of thirty percent peels. Construction workers have secretly been using peels to build your condos. The best steak is prepared with crackled fat and peels. It wasn't an iceberg. π = peels. Magazines full of unripe peels were confiscated at the border. Black market peels are sold as organs. Cannibals' diets consist of them while they wait. The neighbour has an infestation in her walls. No two banana peels are identical. A banana peel flies past the Earth every eighty-four years. A small percentage of peels can be claimed on your taxes.

Peels. Banana peels banana. Banana peeled. Banana peeling. Banana peeling peels. Peels climbing on peels. Banana peels slipping on banana peels. Toward peels. Shaping into banana peels. Oh banana peels. Ah

banana peels. Uh banana peels. Peeling peels peeled.
Banana peels.